A. N. Irvano was born in California in 1990, and
continues to live in the area.
This is the author's second novel.

Falling Horse Books

Falling Horse Books

Lone Wolf Skinny Dipping
Copyright © 2014 A.N.Irvano
First Edition
Book Design: A.N. Irvano

ISBN: 978-0-9960346-1-6
Library of Congress
Printed in the United States of America.

LONE WOLF SKINNY DIPPING

by A. N. Irvano

"Mistakes are the portals of discovery."
-James Joyce

Chapter one

My thumb was out before my feet were fully planted on the ground. Small piles of grey dust kicked up on the faded, chalky tarmac next to me. I smiled as I breathed in the scene. The wind pushed grit, tumbleweeds, and people like me, standing on the periphery. People hoping to leave after their hearts had, at first, been touched, but later, hurt, by the somber living.

A car drove past, but I didn't point or smile to attract their attention. I stood solemnly with only my forearm and hand out, thumb flexed.

My heart leapt out of my throat at the way a heart could be cut. Just next to the valves and atop capillaries, I had been cut.

"I'll be picked up by whoever wants to pick me up," I said to myself as the vehicle kicked up small pellets of rubble past me. I breathed the scene in again. A car's honking behind me shook it slightly. My thumb went down to turn to look. The driver waved an arm and the honks endured. I smiled at my luck.

I liked the persistence, the hot or cold wait in the elements for the anticipation to end and a ride to begin. I hauled my bag out of the bushes and balanced it with my run to the car. I waved and laughed to make sure they didn't get cold feet and try to warm up on the accelerator. The handle of the door was hot, so I opened it fast and got in.

I was working off of an old notion I had when I was young: the 'try everything once' notion. I was young, but not naive -that I inadvertently grew into-

and I knew that all of the things I was going to try, I could only do once and while I was young.

And so, I did the odd jobs I had glorified as a kid. I tried out working in the dirt and mud to see that I loved it. I tried handling wood and metal fittings as a carpenter. I became homeless for a month to be able to know what it was.

I didn't have the bad choices that led me there as many others did. Unsound glamorizations often endure, and my young mind was no exception. I had the image of the New York reporter that had become homeless for a month to capture and understand the underbelly of the world in my head. Like any sheltered and educated person, chaos was a novelty to me. I idealized it. It was a false idea, truly, but before I knew that, I kept it close to my chest, enduring to idealize what shouldn't be.

An idea wouldn't keep the cold away at night. The cold had a way to it; it shifted and grew to take on every painful form it could, then worsened even more. I learned its courses throughout the night. There was no novelty in the hurt of sitting on the street, then setting up a bed in the bushes, then waking up. To only have that to do was pain. I created an organization of the pain. It became turmoil that I grew to know well enough to condition myself to the times and presence of it.

Friendship and camaraderie were to be found in great amount. Comfort in those was a finger away at all times for the homeless network wants no ill to befall it. If another fellow was lacking supplies, they were brought out from a secret hiding hole or burrow, and given. If a couple looked tired on the street, they were offered a bedroll by a man just as weary.

I didn't feel proud, I felt afraid of being found out. To be cast as one of You People that can't walk with the rest of society was shameful. It was made to be. It was loved by middle America to remember there was a Hell on earth and it was homelessness. As long as there are homeless, they will be looked down upon from warm windows of the housed.

I felt good after that month, but it was only a month and I called a cafe, got a job, and stayed huddled under a roof. There, bills being given in exchange for occupying space was an applied concept.

"Oh, hello! You look so beautiful, I just had to get you off of the road!" said the stranger, brown eyes twinkling as they inspected me.

"Yes?" I asked with a steady tone. Good to know the days I didn't look so good were the ones when I shouldn't hitch the hike.

"Oh, yes!" He exclaimed and it took a flicker of my eyes to the road to let him know there was a road, he had a car, and that he should be driving. He nodded and plunged the car forward. We exchanged names but were pretty close to silent. Golden grain shot out of my peripherals and I let my eyes pass over the window pane of the passenger side before thinking about the driver again.

When I did, he spoke up, "So where are you going?" Not an easy question to answer if you don't have a destination. But it is best to have one when hitching.

"California," I said with a long drawl on that last pair of vowels.

"But," he said looking at me nervously, "we are already in that state!"

I made a mockery of myself, gasping and looking out the window, "It's so beautiful!" I clenched my head with both hands in mock surprise and astonishment.

I was born here, knew the roads and dried-up rivers better than this guy, but was willing to let him think this was a new and beautiful moment for me.

"To think I wanted to be in San Francisco before seeing all of this!" I said, putting my hands to my cheeks and opening my mouth slightly.

He was nearly licking up my faux-revelation, "But we are so close! The city, San Francisco, is in this state," he pointed along the road, jerkily. "I'll take you there!" I smiled softly. I had taken advantage of him without thinking I was. While I thought up a way to simply joke around, I had also gotten my needs met. I felt ashamed as I thanked him for his offer and said I would like to go that way.

"I have to tell you, also," his hands gripped and un-gripped the wheel, "I am shaking," he said and made me shiver in worry, but he continued to say the most blasphemous thing I had ever heard, "I am shaking because of your sexiness."

"You're what?" I was beyond astounded and ashamed. A tumult of adrenaline passed over my body and resurfaced to my brain, which was reeling with emotional dry-heaves. My mind pressed his words out of them, retching the disgust from me. I coughed hard, feigning politeness as I covered my face with my hands.

"You are so sexy, with such a lovely body, it makes me shake so," he looked at me helplessly. He let his hands open on the steering wheel and showed me their sporadic twitching. "Your body is so sexy, it makes me shake."

I was a hero of my own life, or perhaps it was a guardian of mine that spoke through me, that said, "But I have a penis."

His jaw dropped with his desires, "Yes?"

I nodded, painting a facade of pride on my face, "Yep."

"But your breasts," he was unable to push together the image of my own chest on the same body as a penis, "they're perfect!"

I could not speak, but I tucked my lips together and shot my eyebrows up, looking at him pointedly.

"Surgery," he said, finalizing it.

"And a lot of it!" I said, feeling the wedge being hammered in securely with the lie. He was content with the state of my genitals for the moment. I continued to gaze out of the window, a little more preoccupied now.

He hesitated to speak and I continued to avoid his eyes. He couldn't speak unless spoken to, now. I was even more ashamed at myself. Finally, maybe accidentally, I looked out his window and saw the rolling hills on my side had taken malformed shapes, junk piles around the debris of railroads that were no longer a part of the American Dream. When I looked out, he caught my eye and opened his mouth. I decided to be accepting. I just looked at him kindly, ready to hear his story or his thoughts.

He commanded me, "Let me see it,"

"What, my penis?" I thought about all of the labor, money, and pain involved in having this penis as I said, "You want to see my genitals." I intoned an air of betrayal and didn't form the words into a question but a statement.

He looked shocked, "How could I say that?"

I had succeeded. "Yes, how could you?" I asked.

"I am a bad man," he said angrily.

"Are you?" I was his sounding-board now, asking of him what he was asking of himself.

"But you," he said and I did not know what he would say next, "are not bad. Thank you so much." I gasped and he continued, "You have changed my life. Of this, I am sure."

I smiled, saying nothing, trusting in some practicality to all of this to him. He smiled now, too, whereas before he had been looking tormented and tortured. By what, though: another human's ability to look good? Was it that easy for me to spin somebody in a half-circle?

He changed my opinions about abstinence and celibacy and for a good two hours of the drive I considered helping the people I liked by not having sex with them. If this guy was so much better off thinking hard about the reasons not to sexualize me, maybe everybody could. I rationalized my future plans of never letting my genitals touch anything but soap for decades to come, foreseeing a great helpfulness abound in me. It would abound in others. Errs of ways would be seen. Men and women would stand taller, enough to part the heavens with torturous abstinence.

"I feel so good," said the driver next to me. I counted that as serendipitous validation to my master theory that I could cause good. I also counted the miles, wondering when I would jump from the vehicle and onto the thoroughfare to flag down a new ride, perhaps with a kindly mother or a simple student. The driver told me how he sold cell phones. He asked if I wanted to be a business partner.

"I have business in the city," I said, becoming a closed book.

"Yes?" He said, but I didn't play the game and keep chatting. The road got a smell all its own and I told him it always, always smelled like this before the cow pastures that were ahead. After I said that, he smiled and nodded but I remembered the lie I had told him about never being here before. As I had become upset and angry at him for imposing his will on my body, I had forgotten the lie I had told him of never coming to California before. I asked myself why I had done that. I felt so impeded and yet, was the original one to impede on him. I asked to get out at the next turn-in.

"What? Here, not the city?" He asked.

I felt admonishing myself next to him wasn't enough. The side of the road was a much better place to reprimand myself for the lie. I had been here, a simple, honest truth, told earlier would have been better than lying. I wanted out of his car, which he had offered and to which I had not been humbled by.

I didn't want to change his life by jokes and lies. I, myself, was one of the two or both if I thought that I could.

"Yes, here is a good place to stop," I said as he did.

He was trying for eye contact, "I want to let you know, again, what a good thing you have been to me."

His eyes sparkled as they had when they had first looked at me. I was disgusted with him as much as myself and said nothing. My bag was already on my shoulder and out of his car with me by the time he caught his breath to continue to get an explanation from me. I walked away, trying to be casual as I did so but feeling the repressing weight of my own misdeeds against my tread.

I never even thanked him, I thought as his car sucked rocks off of the ground and against itself during the pull-away.

I sat on my bag with my thumb out for moments that didn't matter. I let moments of reflection be commonplace, for they often slipped from trivial to notable if given enough time.

The peace and monotony of life, when I had the house and worked in the cafe, was too much to bare. There were inner pains that needed a familiar love it had lost years ago. I began to love quietly until my mind screamed her name for every moment of my life. Finally and fortuitously, I was commended for my love.

Though it was a requited love, I began apologizing to her, I began to say, "I'm sorry," when really what I was saying was, "I'm sorry I ever met you." I was told I was magic, then touched like I was tragic. I woke up to find I had stopped loving and it was better than dreaming. They say you fall in love with the people that remind you of the first person you loved. If that is true, I'll be falling in love with Lane for the rest of my life.

"Travel again," my father had suggested, "you're a young woman, you have a world of possibilities at your feet," he said over the phone and I smiled wanly, thinking about how naive that really was, but he was my dad and had raised me as a single-parent for such a long time that I didn't fault him for what he didn't know about what it was to be a girl, anymore. "That and you've been working so hard, give yourself a break," he had continued.

And it was true, I had been working hard at the job. It was justified to set sail and leave.

I was an empty shell after falling out of love. I barely had my own impulsion. I did the first thing I was urged to do. My dad had known that I had to leave, to rid myself of the strange way love can free you, then at once, shackle you. I emancipated myself from the person that could love her, the town that held her, a sun that could shine on her.

I met stranger after stranger as I set my backpack between my feet, gave a big grin, and extended my hand like I was in a corporate meeting with a new client. I was all too aware of the new judgements I might face from the next stranger. Their cognition mixed with emotions might be a lively match or a grueling and cruel example of the human's inability to hone their own perception. The ability to forget their humanity was humanity's greatest achievement.

It was a scary thing to do, but it was a great distraction. I was self-reflecting and in the moment. I had no worry about getting my head in any number of friends' beds or couches. I didn't want to do things I was unaware of; I didn't want to use them.

Finally, selfishness persisted and the need for water and waste came, so I pulled myself up and put that thumb out hard, signaling all of the vehicles, save patrol cars, which I waved to precociously. The fencing around me was tired and rusted, but I stood on its poles with my thumb out and counted to three-digit numbers as I walked along it before getting down and trying to hitch on the road again.

Just as before, I heard bellowous honking and turned around to see an 18-wheeler pulled over. I grabbed my bag and ran to them with arms up in the air. I entered the cab with a new air of gratitude.

"Thank you, in advance, for the ride!" I shouted happily as I looked up to the driver.

"I couldn't let such a pretty girl stand on the side of the road like that," he smiled and jerked my door to close.

My heart sank but I said, "Thank you."

"I've never picked up a hitch-hiker," he said.

"Oh?" Maybe I could find in this man the human condition to feel compassion. Maybe I could foster it, understand it. I liked that this man had done something out of kindness for me, something that he had never done before.

He sensed his importance and kept talking, "None as pretty as you, of course." He then went on to explain that he was his company's best driver and that his father had taken him down to a "Boy's Town" in Mexico to have his virginity taken, almost in the same mile.

"I would love to have the chance to show America to you," he foamed at the mouth trying to talk. "To have you," he shot a side-long glance in my direction as he spoke, "with me across this continent..." his train of thought ended inside of his own head instead of voiced to me.

"What would you show me?" I was checking the cab's height from the road. I rationalized that I would have to jump onto another car to get out of this vehicle while it was moving if I wanted to be free.

He thought, too, "There are some sites in the Dakotas. Yosemite is one place, too." He smiled again and raised his hand like he was going to put it on my knee. I sought his eyes with mine and shook my head, no. He smiled while placing his hand back on his lap, then, frowning, put it on the wheel.

"You're a good Christian girl. I can tell," he told me.

I sucked in air to reply quickly, "Thanks, the Bible is a part of a subcategory of fallacies called Tautology. The Bible is the word of God. We know this because the Bible tells us so. Sometimes I worry my entire life I've had a number of red herring and non sequitar fallacies stacking up, so I'm not immune."

"Have you ever heard about Sodom and Gomorrah?" he didn't wait for my answer and said, "Two towns burned to the ground by God's angels because the citizens inside were getting too frisky and only one family survived. Would be nice if that sort of thing happened here. A little bit of fire raining down…"

He trailed off but I knew better than to talk. To talk about my atheistic upbringing, my admonishment of religion as it stood. Those were all things he wanted to never understand.

I did say, "God tends to put forth a righteous path for followers."

"Oh, yes, he does!" He looked proud of me. "Now don't go Roman Catholic on me," he intoned.

"Why?" I smiled like I liked the Vatican. What a nice little country they had, where no woman was allowed to reside. My smile was a sad lie.

"Newest Pope has been saying a lot of things. Things that go against the natural order. Like the food chain has been flipped. Saying things like, 'Gay is okay.'" It sounded like a motto people that were sympathetic to the human condition would use. He opened and spit out of his window while ruminating on the thought. "It's not."

"I tend to see spiritually and sexuality as two very fluid things, always ready to progress past what you thought they could be." I tried to say as he spit daggers of mouth phlegm or chew out of his window.

"You have a nice smile, let me see that smile," he said with a halted, sharp timbre.

When forced to laugh or smile, I'll always really be crying. Painful, it is, to put up a farce for others. I said nothing, looking out the window calmly.

He angled his head toward me and decided to reply to what I had said earlier, "Sexuality is fluid. Huh. You sure are breathing out some colorful nonsense every time you open your mouth. All I know is gay's not okay."

I wanted to think out loud, away from what he was saying. "Some parts of human nature struggle against our theories of ethics, still. We forget that knowing is a process and a product. To know something, like whether gay is or is not okay requires both experience and analyzing that experience objectively." He looked at me as I turned to him and I smiled to him, glad he was letting me speak, "Only when we have done that for everything can we say okay or not okay for one thing. Everything!" I breathed out and laughed, "I haven't experienced everything, yet. I know I can't say if one thing is or is not okay based on my experiences."

"You are so adorable." He spit words at me. "I can just tell you're the type of girl that'll still be good in ten years."

I wasn't glad he had said so. I slumped towards the window, thinking of a Japanese man that dressed himself up every day in the iconic pop culture fashion. When asked why he was so cute to so many, the man said, "If hundreds or thousands of people are calling you cute, you become cute."

Throughout my life, I had seen that I was smart by my actions and endeavors. I had seen that I could move mountains with my mind. But, there was a beauty in me that I could never stop getting told about. I didn't cultivate or want it. I read books and researched and cultivated a mind to live from, instead. I was still told that the only thing I didn't know was how cute I was. Life was masterfully handing me the cards I didn't want in my hand. People called me things I had no want to be. People praised and allowed me to prosper because of a power I wouldn't hold.

My SAT scores and bookshelves and theories were good to talk about, once, maybe, for only a few people. The loud and clear message I was getting from society's compliments was, to, "Be cute." I was given power by those attracted to me and it was taken away when I didn't lick it from their hands. Maybe it was their need, as individuals, to be accepted and attractive to other acceptable and attractive people.

I stretched and yawned and my breasts, being largely used to being alone with me, pushed close to my chin as I did so. At that moment, the truck driver veered into the shoulder a little bit too much for my entire being's comfort. I looked at him, astounded, and he just smiled.

He sighed, looking at me, "You make me feel like I have walked through the pearly gates and my body has gone to Heaven."

I felt unsafe and not just from the predatory nature of sexuality but by how strangers were becoming debilitated drivers from it.

My instincts took over and I began acting to ensure my own safety by saying, "This is a good spot to pull over." I pointed to the shoulder of the road ahead of us.

"Oh yeah?" he asked, bouncing in his chair as he turned in.

"Oh yeah." I grabbed my bag and hopped the long distance down and out before I could hear another word from his breathless mouth.

My feet loved running and my body adjusted to the balance of movement. As I warmed, my hips began to sing songs of praise at the movement I was allowing it. Soon, my shoulders popped in to align and my back tried but strayed as it was carrying a mild load. Lungs gushed out stale air. I ran away from the fears I had on the pocked pavement, but I didn't let my heart think it was moving away from its roots.

The spread of ground in front of me let me see myself running with my dad and dogs while my brothers were behind us, casually walking and waiting for us. His tall, dark head of hair sometimes bobbed far in front of me and was sometimes the goal I passed as I overtook his gait. We would meet up and breathe hard while talking, then make the plans to sprint back before doing it. Sometimes we would breathlessly allow ourselves moments to pass in bliss. Our endorphins were running high and we would remember that smiles didn't take too much effort. Once we had put that first foot on the ground, placing intention there to start the run, we wouldn't find any excuse to stop. I let myself go like that, now, with the idea that I wouldn't stop even when the smile had broken through to my inside.

A gas station popped into my view, its metal roof pushing the sun back to the sky and rusted walls looking like they were continually losing pieces of itself onto the ground. I had crossed a valley away from the asphalt I had started on and was in a small town next to a different interstate. I thought not about whether I would put my thumb up there. Dimly, I thought about the repercussions of my quick experiment in experience.

I wouldn't try something that put me close to people's desires, if I could help it. My pride and body were not hurt, but I felt aggravated and upset hearing the words I had heard those two men speak to me play in my subconscious. No amount of will would completely erase the memories.

Irritated, I stomped my foot against the ground rougher and harder than I was used to and my toes caught against a rock as they tried to lift up. I didn't keep running horizontally, but began falling laterally. My palms and knees were against the brown dust of the top layer of dirt. Exhausted now, I looked down at the ground longingly. To know that that is where you'll end up sleeping in a moment of suffering like this can make a person want to forget about pushing against the ground and getting back up. I shook that feeling off, knowing not to think of it, anymore.

I pushed myself up, no longer feeling the pulse of my heart pushing blood to the dots of open, bloody, flesh on my left palm but my head, now. I shook it slightly and adjusted my bag. I pushed down my clothes and worked to pass myself off as something other than a sweaty girl as I stepped over the gas station's parking-lot border.

As I stood in line, the clerk repeated the words of the customer in front of me, saying, "Thirty-three on number five!" She said both numbers with such enthusiasm, it impacted me almost immediately.

I thought of my dad saying, "It's not what you say, but how you say it," and what that meant here. The clerk said it so energetically that I couldn't help but be happier. What she said, a number, a very abstract and arbitrary thing, just needed an uplifting intonation to denote happiness: an important emotion to be forcing on another.

The clerk looked me up and down, then said, "Well you must be able to breathe underwater."

I asked, "What do you mean?"

"You're sweating so much, she said, then added, "I just had to make a joke about it before I start pushing daisies. You have to have fun while you can, am I right?"

She swiped my coffee and baguette as I placed a chocolate bar on the counter, saying, "You're right,"

She giggled and said, "Some things are just worth it, huh?"

I winked at the chocolate, "Most certainly are."

The customer behind me was not as joyous and pushed me, grumbling as he did.

The clerk admonished him, "Don't start spitting fire out of the puddles you've been crying, Larry." I jumped aside, watching the transaction while peeling back the plastic on my candy.

"Liquid fire, for you?" she said as she rung it up. "Well, this can freeze up any problems you're having." She looked up at him, but his body remained rigid and she went on, "It'll get through just about anything." He took the red bottle and left past me, sidestepping me as he gave me a faint smile. She gave some emphasis in saying, "Have a good day!" When he left, she said to me, "Sorry about Larry, he used to do some of the drugs and, well, just hasn't been the same since. He could use some lavender instead of all that cocaine rolling through his system." She put her chin to her fist and sighed, "It'd be nice, but heck if it'll happen. Stay safe out there, Miss."

I jumped outside, where I was already chomping into the candy. I used the restroom connected to the gas station and followed the silt and rubble path next to it down to a stream. The coffee was small and meshed with my already-warm throat and stomach well. As I opened and closed my mouth many times to eat down the baguette sandwich, my mind raced me up and down the stream as many times.

Once I was done eating, I didn't think to take my shoes and socks off and wade up it. I just did it, like a system of work your body and mind have done for months, I pushed forward into it. They both start talking, your body and mind, and acting without conscious thoughts asking or telling. That's how I got into the stream, placing my feet and toes into cracks and dips in rocks to push past the smooth, mossy tops that wouldn't let me propel off of them, in a way both thoughtful and thoughtless.

Back home, we called this spelunking in the crick. Creek sounds like crick when you have red on your neck from sun and those pinching, wriggling crawdaddies in your hands. I smiled joyously as I placed my feet among the browned algae and reeds of one pool and that smile took me way up the waterway. Underneath a one-lane bridge there was a sun-speckled pooling of the freshest water I had splashed through yet. I peeled off the already-wet clothes I was wearing and propped my bag against a rock before letting myself lay back and float.

The sun warmed my entire torso and legs and, soon, face. I reveled in the leaves overhead creating intricate layers of branches and trees to produce patterns and mesmerizing illusions. Softly focusing in on the leaves, then out on the wider picture, then back on the leaves, I thought of Mesmer, an eighteenth-century Austrian physician that was the first to use hypnotism, calling it "animal magnetism." If he were to see me, a lone wolf, looking up at the trees, mesmerized while skinny dipping, he could have been, for once, a well-proven man.

I had no better physician present than myself and I decided to get out of the water and onto a warmer, higher, and dryer surface before nightfall. I changed into toastier clothes and dried my hair a bit. I thought of the Dutch proverb: The hardest part of the journey is getting one foot out the door.

Like my father and I had done, I had hit my foot against the pavement and started. Forgetting all of the things I could do in a home or school, I thought of all of the things I would do out of them and never looked back. This part, the observing of all that is beyond a doorstep, was the part to be enjoyed.

It was less joy that I had found to be the product I was looking for, so much as learning. If I were to inspect that joy, I might be able to see its foundations were made by a home that valued school and a school that valued learning. I could see, as I lay in the fully warming sun and tepid water, that there was an abundant ignorance about me. Knowing you are empty of something, though, is only the first step to filling it, not the last.

Without asking, thoughts swarmed around the causal relationships between the men driving and me in my head. I had been the first to ask them for rides with my upturned thumb, and they had, in turn, asked me for what they wanted. Imposing on them my desires, had I allowed them to do the same, or did neither of us have a right to ask too much of the other? Both of the men had been hurt by me, in ambiguous ways, by my rejection of them. They, though, had hurt me by forcing me to reject them, hadn't they? Whether I had really hurt them at all was an argument I could force myself to have, as well.

The droning buzz of these questions, like bees both destroying and populating the flowers in my mind, created a noisiness I couldn't slap out of my ears. Water that had collected in them from my lackadaisical swim aggravated the feeling until I had lured myself away from them. I massaged my shoulders and upper back as far as I could reach. On my run I had loosened the knots I had made while having that power of beauty handed to me and taken away by those two drivers. Now that those knots were undone, I had a strong yearning to unbridle myself of them completely.

More of what I had gone through today would not be in tomorrow's plan. I wanted to be alone, for to be alone is to be with every person I had ever known.

I knotted a strap on my backpack, thinking about letting it carry me to the backwoods around these parts. I at least wanted a day or two of solitude, to not hear my own voice pierce the quietude. To not need to think long and hard about the places syllables and vowels were pushing me, for the time it took the sun to return twice above my head would be the bandage I needed now.

I had some essentials and could get through one night or two before picking up more extensive supplies and equipment. A survival book had told me humans are tropical beings, so unless you're in the tropics you'll need extra warmth and shelter beyond your skin and bones and whatever pile of sticks you're calling your dwelling. I thought about the mud and tools I would need to make a home out of a haystack. This wasn't about to be another bout of prompted houselessness, this was about to become a bout of homesteading in no-man's land.

I made plans and thought about what they meant. I had to be both greater than my goals and humble enough to think they were greater than me. I proposed hatchet or machete debates to myself as I climbed the hill above the stream, a tough and scratchy ascent compared to crick spelunking. My palms pressed into my thighs and then gripped earth as I pulled myself up the deepest part and then onto the dirt next to the guardrails of the road. I would use a hatchet in these piney woods, definitely, I thought as I picked my way up past the creek.

Chapter Two

A white Toyota with bales of hay in the bed and a horse-tow was bubbling along the bridge's berth. I gripped the guardrail, ready to hop it, run across, and continue climbing the mountain after the truck had passed.

Perhaps sensing something more as he saw me, the driver moved his right arm as he shuffled the clutch and stopped. The lone wolf that would like to live passionately and without restraint in me was rolling its eyes at what it saw as another intrusion.

"Heya," he said.

"Yeah?" I was getting an instinct to be polite with him, but I disregarded it and was trite, "Can I help you?"

He smiled at what he must have known was not earnestness and said, "Actually, I didn't know I was going to get a horse at auction, but I did." He laughed towards his passenger seat and continued, "I thought I was going to lease my mare to a friend. When he backed out last minute at the county show, I found myself putting down a few grand for this guy." I was going to look, peek in, just to see, but I didn't want to allure to my animalistic tendencies by looking at his. He may have the opportunity to see the longing in my eye and stab me in the back while I was goggling. I put a hand on my right hip and pushed it up.

"I have two mustangs now, you see my problem? They are a match made in," he looked down, "get what I'm saying?"

I did, I understood, but what to say back I did not know, "You look, above anything, like a strong girl, and," he paused and stopped to look at me, "You are a horse person, are you? Not scared of them are you?" The horses both snorted and my eyebrows went up, I was done pretending. I shook my head and looked at them intently. Both were strong in their faces and let their sharp eyes fixate on me.

"Oh no, I'm not scared of them." I continued to watch him, though. "I'd love to help with them, any way I can." The ways I could help looked minimal compared to what he could do, though. He had small grey hairs popping out of the pores all over his face, except for his nose and forehead. Weathered and army-tattooed arms showed me he was both a veteran and a farmer. His hat sat above his entire head and gave room for the leather strap that held all of his gray and white hair back in a bundle.

The man shook my hand, "Robert."

"Ashna," I said tilting my head toward him, realizing nobody else had thought to ask.

"Damn that's prettier than you are!"

I laughed, trying to focus attention away from narcissism, "A terribly great number of things are."

"You're a smart one. If I had a daughter it'd be nice if she were smart like you..." he really let the statement hang in the air, over the idle of his engine and the stamping of hooves behind him. His revery was not self-contained as he really looked me in the eyes, saw something in my soul, and just touched it with the curl of his smile into those dewy eyes.

"So you know anything about horses?" He started to empty his passenger seat, placing things around a border collie that sat up tall next to him.

"Not too much, but just enough." I replied as I went around to the other side. In front of his truck I thought about the prospect that this was a continuation of what had happened earlier. I persevered, though, listening to an instinct to try, just one more time.

"It is special, the way you came up to me without me asking you for anything," I said, finding the difference enlightening.

"Now don't think I'm weird or anything like that." I nodded, knowing that was one of the thoughts I had to hold onto and he continued, "I've been this way ever since I married my wife, Lucy, years ago. I won't do anything that isn't from the kindness of my heart, don't worry."

"You're probably just as kind as she is," I thought of his gift-offer to me and started wondering more about it. The words came out of his mouth in a genuinely loving tone when he spoke and something in me had changed and become more trusting.

I said, "You can be worried about everything but the right things to be worried about, in fact, most people are. I try not to decide what to worry about, these days."

He spoke what I was looking to hear, "I was just worrying while I was driving along, thinking about how I won't have two bulls on the property nor will I have two mustangs. I think how I'd like a horse person to walk up to me and say, Bob, I need myself a ride, and go on and give him this horse I've built up these past ten years."

"Just give it?" I asked speculatively.

"Gifting economy here, Ashna. Did I say it right?" I nodded and he smiled, "Good."

He patted the steering wheel and said, "I didn't know I'd want a whole solar panel set-up, but last year I got gifted a whole ten panels. Enough to take me off the power company. A whole year without bills and I can go to town and buy a horse without thinking once about it. It's really nice." He chewed his lower lip speculatively and the white patch of beard under it jutted out horizontal. "I wonder what you will be like a year after this horse," he said to me. He didn't look at me, but his eyes sparkled in a way I had never seen. I thought that what he said was awfully auspicious, as what ought to happen doesn't always happen. I might be destined to do well investing in some tiny firm in San Francisco tomorrow or I might be destined to build a house in the woods near his house.

I had no idea what ought to happen, but I knew his goodwill and good intentions were not two things to let get trashed and tossed up like a weed on the highway.

"This is Chloe, by the way," he patted his dog and she stood up, wagged that tail, and sat down again as he said her name. "Never bought a horse before. I, myself, roped White Stripe, the horse you might want. This mare, Gilda, is my wife's. New horse's name is..." he opened a pocket notebook and said, "Nostradamus."

I laughed, "Predictable."

"Not quite," he said and we both trailed off in thought for a few moments.

"Where is home?" I asked.

"Montana," he smiled. I did, too. He put on country tunes and asked me about school and what I had enjoyed studying.

I was enthusiastic and he asked softly, "Why was it you didn't finish up college?"

I sighed, becoming a little more vulnerable and relaxed, "I had started when I was fifteen. College classes every other day, a few hours of high school the other days. I got burnt out a few months after graduating high school." He nodded and rubbed the top of Chloe's head. "I wanted to see if there was a place for what I was learning in society. There was, but not one that fit me in with it."

"Some of the best stuff I know has been handed down," he said, "like companion planting or what to and to not plant next to one another. Everything has order and place and reason but not all of that is taught in books. A lot of that stuff is taught orally and through doing it. It's just your place as a being to find them out."

"Knowing something and applying it are two different things," I mused.

"Oh, so you can know to plant things a certain way, but if you don't go out there and put in the hours and sweat it won't matter a damn!" He added, "Not everything is good to know either."

"Yeah. And when you know something about the way your neighbor acts, you haven't bettered your neighbor, you've bettered yourself." I said, "Nothing you can do about other people."

He cornered carefully around the mountain road and sighed, "Comes a time when you realize you can't change the world, just work on making yourself a better place."

"I could make a real nice place without the whole world trying to interfere and impose on me," I said, holding my cheek with my hand and looking outside.

"Don't go hiding in a hole, neither," he jibed his finger towards me.

I shrugged, "I'd like to, after today."

He laughed, "But when you get that nice place inside yourself you must be humble and honest enough to show the world who you are. Be a role model to those that don't have what you do. Be noble!" He had crow's feet above his beard and deep creases on either side of his nose down into the tufts of his grey and white hair. He munched on his own bottom lip and his beard jutted outward, making harsh angles of his profile. I noticed his long hair slung behind his tan ten-gallon hat and it inspired thought.

I said, "Native Americans say they leave their hair long if the win all of their battles."

"I haven't fought in a long time. Besides, I'm no Native. I can't take their rites and values as mine if I'm not helping them or one of them, can I?" he looked at me and asked with a shaking timbre of his voice, "You fight?"

"I think I'm trying to stop," I heard myself saying. I stroked my hair down my shoulder and past my collarbone, idly thinking.

He patted his dog and laughed out, "There is no try, little missy. Only do." He laughed abruptly, "My Toyota likes it when I quote Yoda. Yes you do, you little Toyota Yoda." He brushed the vinyl dash and patted it sweetly, "Yes, you do."

"I'll learn." I listened to my words loose tenacity as I talked.

"You don't have to learn one more gosh-darned thing." He adjusted his hat and the sling around his hair. "You gotta just do. You are right now!"

I nodded.

"What do you want?" he asked.

"Nothing," I opened my hands to show they were empty.

"What can you have?" he asked.

"Everything," I said, hands open to whatever fell in my lap.

He whistled praise,"I'll be gosh-darned if my wife don't love you."

I tingled at the statement. If she didn't, what would become of me? I let my doubts vanish as I sought sight of the sun. It was setting behind the dark green pines, splashing together a pink and yellow background to their stark lateral lines and fuzzy horizontal branches, both deep black. The drive was one of patience and it was past dark by the time we had driven up to his metal gate, flanked by two wooden redwood stumps and not much else to my eyes, since very little was illuminated past the headlights.

"Wait right inside the gate while I open it and take these two inside. Might be a good minute." He took a key off of his caribiner and got out of the truck. I did, too, leaving my bag in his car while I moved close to the gate. He tipped his hat and was a silhouette in the headlights for a moment before unlocking the gate, pushing it hard to the left of the truck. The horses were whinnying and as he pulled the horse trailer and vehicle past me, he pointed in the distant darkness.

He said, "There's a post with a halter, lead rope, etcetera out there. Go say hi to ol' White Stripe. See if it's a match, you know what I'm saying."

I nodded and ducked beneath the fence poles and began walking in the dark, hands in pockets. I could hear the rumble of his engine as he led his truck to a lit barn a football field away. The night's fog was slowly beginning to stifle the air in my lungs. Around me, it felt like I was swimming instead of walking. I heard a shrill whinny as I stubbed a toe against protruding dirt clods, and looked hard in the dark. I gave a human's whinny back to him. The ground became more apparent around me as the fog rolled away from the moon and it illuminated more around me. He snorted in reply and the bob of his head as he did so brushed out of the darkness and to a place where I could see him. A white stripe, ebbing closer in the darkness' water, was what I saw first. I clucked to him like I would to any animal and I heard his hooves beat against the dirt as he trotted. My feet felt the vibration on the ground like they were soaking in the trembling of pavement after loaded trucks pass along it. In that paddock, I felt the horse's power pushing against his home turf to approach me.

His white stripe bobbed in the night's darkness. I saw two quick glints of his eyes above him as he sailed through the black air to me. I breathed so he could hear me and moved my hands slowly. He placed his head in front of me, breathing like me and was quick to accept my hands around his nose and mouth. He bobbed his head and I let go, ready to both dodge him and let him put his head closer. He chose to have me do the latter as he pushed his open mouth across my collarbone and over my shoulder. A trail of his saliva on my skin was quick to prick to the cold. My hands wanted to brush it off, warm it, but to do so might spook him. Instead, I was not quick with my movements and hands but methodical.

He pushed his head back and bobbed it up and down before stamping a hoof. I put my hands on his forelock above his face, onto his mane, down his neck, then to his chest, and down on to rub his shoulder. I sidestepped and was parallel to him, facing away from his head and was pushing my weight into him. An act of balance ensued, where he pushed back and then let me do so too until he held his mass up with just three legs. I lifted his front right hoof up and inspected it. It had a clean middle frog, intact edges, and no signs of stress. I checked the rest with the same findings, put a hand on his back to see he didn't shy from pressure, and began to swipe off extra dirt, hair, and skin from him. The best way to approximate height is with your hands from above the shoulder on the withers, down.

"Fifteen, eh?" I said, "That'll do, White Stripe." He nickered gently and nudged me with his nose.

My bones ached a bit from the drives I had been on to get to him. My muscles were cold, too. I made a show of clapping my hands on my legs and then shoes, seeing if I was right in assuming he wouldn't spook. He didn't flick his ears or flinch at all; instead, he put his head close to my shoes, inhaling. I gave him a pat and rub where his girth would go. I checked to see if he really wasn't a gelding. The stallion bits hung from the end of the velvety soft path of skin and bunny-soft hair. He was a rarity and a gem to lay at a Sultan's step. He was one of the tame mustangs, never neutered but not pawing the air with two hooves and holding onto the ground with two others. What was my perspective if not limited, though. I had only worked with ex-race horses, docile mares and one extremely pleasant draft horse.

I led myself away from him, starting to sing a song about my day at the river and meeting him, a tactic to keep horses calm. I heard the thunderous clapping of his hooves against the dirt as he followed me from behind. The sound of his breath was alluring behind me, but to make him give chase on me was what I wanted. I stopped singing and started running, attuned to the sound of him moving from a trot and starting to a canter next to me.

I was running again, like I had had both feet out the door a long time before being here. It had taken a great deal of learning to get here and to feel this moment and to let it envelope me in it. I felt surrounded by the pleasure in front of me, free of any plan but to gently grasp this feeling and remember it; when I thought of the past's pain or the future's limitations I could recall the hot feeling of the mustang's breathe on my neck while cold, wet grass whipped at my ankles and shins and I would smile, again. I smiled and laughed to him and could feel his breathing shorten, like small chuckles were escaping from his clattering teeth.

The clapping of hooves next to me slowed as we approached a pole and tack shed next to the stark white wood of the gate and a grooming stand. I put my hand on his face, over the white stripe and chestnut hairs, while grabbing the halter and lead. He nuzzled into my hand and I looped the halter on and over his face, forelock, and ears. I led him out the gate. I remembered on the second try the looping to get the perfect releasable knot and hitched him up. I groomed him with curry comb and hog-hair brushes. I picked a bit of mud and grass out of his hooves and looked around for a bridle.

"Which one's yours?" I asked White Stripe. There were only two bridles and, remembering the mare was docile, knew his was the one with more bit hooks and snaffles than the other, "I don't really like your bridle. It looks like it hurts." In the darkness he pawed the dirt beneath him solemnly and stretched his neck to nibble on the new plant growth there.

"It wouldn't be going too far to take a few of them snaffles off, then," came Robert's voice in the night. He had his wife's mare next to him and he tied her lead up to the pole I had done my fancy knots on.

"Well, all right, then!" I said as I untied leather fastenings on the bit pieces of the bridle. I studied its size with my thumb and index finger and compared it to White Stripe's face, then adjusted based on the differences. I could hear Robert removing his mare, Glenda's, leg-wraps and whistling as he did it. Swooping bats and owls playing in the night's grey matter scared the mare. I looked around for them as they swept in and out of my vision.

"I have a bridle path we can walk down together, but as for her, she needs a night to rest her bones. Oh, Glenda." He tapped her on the shoulder with a curry comb, "I can just tell that you don't ride Western saddles, Ashna."

I nodded, "Right, but I have converted a few horses to English before. I can pick one up in town when I get more supplies."

He looked at me and I back at him. It must have been a harvest moon just before spring, because I could see his face clearly. I thought then about why I hadn't noticed it and flicked my eyes to look round at the illumination. He swung his body to look at it, too, before speaking.

"Now I haven't let a soul nor a physical body besides my own and my wife's touch this horse because I love him so goodness-gracious much. Now you don't go lounging around on him. You go see the country with him. Really push him, he can take it."

"Well, I can do that," I complied. "I would love to do that."

"Don't buy a saddle in town. I have spare English equipment," he brought out one from the tack shed, "that you can have. Now the farrier's just come and he's had those shoes in for a few weeks now and they're not as soft and flexible as they could be, just in case you're going to need to take him on the big black tarmac, they're solid for that, too." He placed the saddle on his horse as he said this and threw the girth under his belly to my waiting hands.

"Do I cinch it to the third notch? Looks like it." I studied the polished leather. The long strip of girth was the same cherry red as the saddle.

He grunted on the other side of the horse in reply while I worked the leather and metal bindings to fasten everything together. I finished and looked around him to see his face pressed against White Stripe and both of his hands on the horses eyes. Both were in a place all their own, like the lone wolf and the river it skinny dips in, both had formed a non-inherent bond. My hand touched the flank of the horse and an overwhelming feeling of understanding for them came over me. I pressed my face into his mane and both of us humans sighed, satisfied with life without limits. As we pulled away from the horse, he whinnied softly to us, his mare, his past life on a slow farm. Or maybe he was just making a bestial noise.

The bestial magnetism Mesmer talked of was present here, I decided, as I led horse away from man and stepped through the stirrup and onto his back. A normal horse would immediately shift his weight when that extra weight of a human was on him, but he became buoyant, like sailing with strong winds.

"Anything spook him?" I called to Robert.

"Not a thing. Tramples water, faces the wind, and laughs at loud sounds." He added, "You two have a soul connection, a past life thing or something is going on there. I'm going to let him show you around. Come back up that way to the barn and my wife and I will set you up with a place for the night," he said. "Then you and he can be off to see it all, whatever that may be."

"Thank you so much," I wanted to sing to him, now, of gratitude and appreciation but apprehension caught in my throat.

"Count it as a blessing," he advised and I thought about my blessings and just how many I would get. I was counting it as one of them. The horse underneath me counted his new rider as one, too. He gradually tested my boundaries and I responded each time. He would try a new stride and I would adjust variant degrees to it. He was graceful in his actions and, presumably mind, as he carefully found the best way to dance with me along the trail, then intentionally off of the trail, then to a higher trail, then to dance back onto Robert's property and next to the barn. He put White Stripe in a fresh stall inside after slipping the tack off of his back and face.

"There's a good amount of supplies in this bag. His certificated, current test results with a good bill of health, more saddle pads down in there, all kinds of other stuff. Think of it like a magical bag, this one," he patted two bags that sit behind the saddle, on the rear of the horse and then opened up one of the bags, which was empty, "For your personal items. His back can take it, yours can't. I'll get my wife to join us for soup while you shuffle your things. The room and bed for you is up the stairs and the light's already on." He moved out of the barn and I emptied my backpack in an organized fashion, mostly thinking to put my weather resistant clothes and pants I could ride in on top. By the time I was done I was being handed beefy green soup and introduced to Lucy, Robert's love. He was a tall man next her, his hat was off, gray hair was flowing past his collarbone

34

and shoulders, and he was quick with a hand to hold onto his wife when she started sighing, asking him jovially why she had to marry a horse lover turned horse trader.

"Because nobody else had enough guts to get you a pony, Luce," he said amicably.

I chomped the kale in their soup and tasted the recognizable anise seeds, but had to ask, "What's in this soup?"

"Oh, your normal farm soup, except I used a bone broth," Lucy said, eyes glittering as a smile tucked under them.

"I think I like it, thank you for feeding me," I told them, sipping after I did.

"It's quite special, it is," Robert agreed.

"You are welcome, dear," Lucy tilted her head to her shoulder as she said so.

"It's making me quite sleepy, actually. Or perhaps that's the result of my long day, I don't know. Would you two mind if I went to sleep, soon?"

"Of course! Nothing to stop you! But I'll be hoping to see you and this guy," he went over to feed White Stripe more alfalfa, "out of here as soon as the rooster's crowing. Not for much reason, I just want to see you two doing something better than entertaining two old crows while your youth goes to waste."

I nodded, unsurely, and let the last of the soup wash down my throat before handing it to Lucy.

She smiled and returned to another room, probably the kitchen, with it.

"For your benefit, Ashna," he smiled with Lucy, "not mine. You're going to have a great time and there's no use watching two old farmers working while you wait for the right moment. I got you a map out of the closet. In your pack. Trust yourself to use it?"

I trusted myself whole-heartedly. Telling other people that was something I didn't normally do.

There was a great deal happening that I didn't normally do. My mind revolted, trying to make sense of the contradictions I was learning.

Should I tell him and his wife what a shock I was going through? Bukowski wrote, "I've been stabbed by so many flowers, I don't know what to do when I'm given flowers. It takes time," and I felt that helped me be patient. I didn't have to understand everything right away, I might not even know if I would want to do this tomorrow until I've done it tomorrow, only then can I judge it as a part of my life or not. To feel like I wasn't used to being fulfilled by somebody else; this day was testament enough to that. I could wait and graciously be able to see at a distance how they added to the landscape of my life.

"I can and will!" I said and thought, Thank you! I turned myself in to bed and let my mind wander in its wonders while I fell asleep.

I woke up to hear rooster and the sounds of White Stripe pawing the wood on his stall, beneath my head. I woke myself up quickly, made the bed, and hopped down the stairs to brush my teeth and put boots on. He was alone and I gave him an apple to munch on as I re-checked his hooves, wrapped his legs with some flannel wraps I saw poking out of the saddle-bag to warm him up, and saddled him up.

White Stripe whinnied just before I put his bridle on and I placed my hand on his forehead. He breathed softly on me and I felt the pull of the wind outside lift his mane. I breathed in the fresh morning air as I pushed the bridle up his face and unto his mouth. I surprised myself by not waiting and deciding to jump into the saddle to ride out right there in his barn-stall. He happily walked out with me on his back. Fog tendrils swooped past us and I saw layers of it split apart and regroup. Between his shoulders and tail, I sat confidently. We set off at a trot to the gate, where Robert stood. He was holding a coffee mug to his chest and seemed to have the same patience I was looking to attain.

"Now that I see you two ride, I absolutely know you're meant for this," he esteemed.

"Thank you, sir," I began.

He cut me off, "Now get going on seeing the beauty that is this land," I nodded harshly and wanted to salute. "Where you going?" he asked.

"No idea. I thought I knew everything but I am wrong," I enthused.

He said something I had never heard, "You seem a sad, sad girl. What makes you that way?"

"I guess I used to think the world was exactly as it should be. Now I know that's not the case."

"Then what do you want?" I remembered how I had answered yesterday but felt my answer was different now.

"I wish the world was a different place," I thought about it and became bemused with the beauty the world could potentially hold, "I really really wish for that," I said.

"Well, then I really really wish for you to get just that," he said and whistled. White Stripe snorted happily and Robert opened the gate, whistling to him. White Stripe took a trot's gait and clipped past the gate, fencing, and pasture. The way ahead was foggy and I turned back to take a good look at Robert and the farm he lived on, but he was gone and fog swirled over the house and barn and sweeping meadows that were there. Even the place where the old mare and new stallion were was a rolling layer of white.

CHAPTER THREE

We drove ourselves into the fog bank ahead of us, the two of us. It harnessed White Stripe no more than the bridle could, but held me like a harness would. I felt an irrevocable stiffness come with the mist. We passed through the layers of dense fog. It was thick like steam from a pot of pasta that I had just opened, it pushed me back. The normal properties of gaseous liquid seemed to just leave as the solidity pushed against me. I doubted that I could have even walked through the density of this atypical fog if I had been on foot. While I felt the enormous pressure, White Stripe moved even faster, like a racer following the white line on the middle of the road. As we passed trees and mailboxes, only half of their forms would push out of the whiteness of the fog. The accelerated pace we were going made it impossible to really make out their full forms.

Giant ferns and tall tree branches were able to push gently out of the constraining mist, but only for brief moments. The forms around the road guided my path and reins non-simultaneously; the white murk was still constant. Three layers of insulation on my torso and I could still feel the delicate mist prod and poke my shoulders. When I looked down, I did not see near-invisible globes of water, but pearly white dots form on the parts of my apparel apparent to me. The fog was pulling and pushing my body with immense strength as well as bleaching my clothes as I wore them. I looked back up slowly to see the haze was forming wispy layers and letting sight of emerald green conifers break free of the incongruity that was that dense and bearing fog.

Upon seeing daylight and breaking our last path to freedom, I bent down a bit to pat the horse's neck and say, "My only question now, you magnificent beast." He snorted victoriously, "Is how you just went galloping through that with extreme ease and comfort while I could barely push through it." I said, "Good health, eh?"

I lifted my head and continued us along the road, taking moments to study my outer jacket, which was now white all over. The saddle-bags, and the rest of the tack he was wearing, were still their respective cherry and mahogany colors. I watched as around us, the forest's layer of fog decreased and wild layers of trees and ferns collaborated. Growth over growth over generations produced a myriad of patterns and answers to questions only the blue surface of my eyes had access to.

I noticed as we turned to run down the mountain that my horse's body was moving like he was going up a hill. But all butt and back leg effort was going into getting us down. I sat atop, unable to know if I should sit like he was going down or up. His back angled up and I was able to sit like going up a flat while we roller coaster cruised down the mountain hill.

I shook the feeling and breathed a bit as we flew down and towards the first city. As we entered, flames licked out of a small shed. White Stripe shied away but steadied when I asked him to. I had seen something extraordinary, and I wanted to see it closer. The new flame from the shed was liquid matter in front of me, moving up and down and to the sides, licking out in some places, and bounding with energy in others. It was not dying away as it moved. I would approximate that it had reached its pique, then stopped moving or taking up any more energy at all.

In a very quick instant I felt like a foreigner in a land that I thought would be much more hospitable.

Paris syndrome, commonly featured among people from Japan going to Paris. There was a disparity between what they had been told and what they got. When the tourists entered Paris, they bega` n to experience hallucinations, delusions, or dizziness. They suffered the syndrome while seeing the realistic Paris, after having an idealistic view of the city in their hometown. The cure was going back home.

But I did not.

Going back home, it was beyond what I wanted to do. The sadness, the weakness I had there. It was unapproachable.

I advanced towards the churning liquid fire stealthily and grabbed a long, thick branch in one hand. I approached it even closer, seeing that it was concrete and rigid, yet still moved and shifted as fire could. I poked the solid fire with the branch. When I looked at the wood it was icy and charred with freeze.

"I've seen enough." I shouted as I approached my steed to board him and leave, "Do you agree?" I looked at him, jerkily, and scared. He breathed that in through flared nostrils and looked at me as though his temper were rising, eyes wide and head raising upwards and away.

"Ho pony and quiet down, it'll be all right." I stroked him and as he calmed down, thought about what would benefit us, "Let's just bottle up some of this."

I shuffled in the saddle-bag and pulled out a large canteen and a tiny metal spoon. I placed it around a lick of the material flame matter, and scooped it in with the spoon. I dropped the tiny spoon twice because it grew chilled the longer I held it to the flame. I put the canteen in my jacket's pocket and the spoon back in the bag, happy to have it out of my hands as it worked to numb them with cold. I looked to the fire once more, thinking it was solid, then liquid, but definitely knowing it wasn't a gaseous inferno. No, by the way it was moving it wasn't gas, at all but a solid, or perhaps liquid. It was mesmerizing because I couldn't quite make sense of it.

I clicked at him with my mouth to turn, get the other way around, then out- but he wouldn't turn and led me at a new type of gallop than I was used to down the hill and towards a waterfront. I was so affronted with him and his lack of concession to my dominance that I thrust my feet into his sides at the first sign of his lack of confidence, to which he reared and pawed the ground, then jumped from the shore, down.

The best idea I had was to grab at the canteen in my pocket and open it onto the water dozens feet down. If fire can freeze other matter and solidify in open air, what will it do when added to water? I asked myself these things as I saw the fire ooze quickly out and onto a portion of the surface we were landing on. The canteen and my arms were pushed back as White Stripe and I pushed through the surface of the water, only to be flipped on it and left, rearing up like we were falling down.

We were upside down on the surface of the water we landed on like it was White Stripe's new ground. He struck it and the water splashed from him pawing it like chimes in my ears and he began his unbridled gallop on it.

I would look above and over myself while riding as I might look to the sky, except it was to the sea I looked. The schools of fish that passed above our heads were like clouds drifting in the sky. The seaweed and algae sprouting from the ocean bottom looked like trees and shrubs pushing towards us. The only creatures that came near us were dolphins. Their shrill As we galloped closer towards the forests of kelp, the enormity of the deep, unsettling indigo sea that was now our sky became a heavy, immense, and unbearable weight.

Though it was unusual, I accepted it readily and didn't allow my doubts to stop what we were set to do. I thought this hard running a good activity of the soul. I likened us running on the underside of the water's surface to trusting a road that we could be on. We weren't hitting many bumps, divots, or potholes, we were riding smoothly. It was meditative and we ran the great length of water, above its great depth.

When put in a blackened room with only one light, participants in a study would begin to see the light move, but only because of an illusion the individual eye was making- a kind of way of sustaining looking at a bright light that long was to shove it to a different part of the eye. It was called the auto kinetic effect and was a complete illusion.

Illusions like that happen in the everyday, yes. Illusions help us cope.

When a group was put in that blackened room, with a fixed light that seemed to move to them, the participants talked about where the light moved and conformed to a group estimate. Physiologically, it was impossible for everyone to see the same thing as their eyes were moving the light away from the same point sporadically. Even when faced with illusions, we as people still have a need to coalesce.

"Now that I see you from this lens of mine, sea," I said, chatting after hours of riding with my surroundings, "I'm upside down and on only your shallow bit, but I do, I see why the abysmal dark is called an abyss." I wondered as to what had created this, if not a patterned, quantifiable thing.

I slowed White Stripe to a trot before we came to a sandy bank slipping towards us. We touched the sand and exited the water. I took off his saddle and sat on the bank, which was wide and splashed with sun. I let White Stripe stay roped up nearby while I closed my eyes for a rest.

The day, which had been so contrary to what I usually experienced, was still a writhing mass in my mind and I was not tempted to add any new experiences to think about. I simply slipped off my boots and sighed as the sun melted the patches of skin that were not covered with clothes.

I was slowly grasping that I had gotten what I had asked for with Robert when I wanted the world to be flipped on its head. Roots were growing in the open-air next to me and flowers were probably growing upside down in the ground. The grass was blue and the sky was more green than blue and maybe, if I ventured forth, people would be nice. That's what would happen if the world really was an opposites one, after all. My eyelids felt the liquefying warmth of the sun and I dozed. I lackadaisically hoped and dreamed but did not want to get up to try just yet. My body had become planted and my eyes only wanted to see the black of their own eyelids.

I dozed there with the stallion for a few hours without thinking against it. I ate a quick meal from the bags and threw him some more of his line, letting him eat even more of the sapphire grass around us. The sun was slower in the sky than I was used to and, instead of packing out tents or tarps to stay the night, I ventured onto my steed and out onto what roads we could find.

Chapter four

We were still close to civilization because I would catch smells of burning stoves and soon we were out of barely cleared land and onto tarmac, the ground of which White Stripe nearly faltered at. We walked slowly along it until a woman came flying out of her house and along the trail from her house to the road. Scarves of many reds and pink hung from her as she ran and licked at her ligaments, the top two of which were holding onto a pie. White Stripe whined that whinny horses do when they want the food they see. I waved joyously as I slowed him to a stop.

She was breathless, "I felt this urge to slice up an apple pie! Then when I look out the window, I see you! Now what is such a beautiful man doing getting himself cut up and hurt?" I had gotten some cuts and scrapes that she was looking at, but they meant nothing to me then; I was more astounded by what gender she was assigning me.

She went on, "Terrible thing, not taking care of beauty like yours."

I shrugged even harder, the weight of the heavy-handed compliment pushing on me was greater than that I felt on the fog-laden road.

"Anyway, here you are," she handed over the sealed-up pie like it was nothing to her. I tried to place it in my bag, but it was cumbersome in any position. I relented to letting it sit in the other saddle bag with my clothes and closed the bag on it. I thanked her.

"For such a handsome man, it really is no problem." I felt her advance towards me and the horse with her body. I lunged back and I felt White stripe lose confidence under me. I tried to reclaim me emotions.

"That really does mean a lot to me, your compliment," I stammered, "but, I don't think you see me clearly, see." I trailed off and she smiled brightly.

"Oh, I see what I want," she said absolutely ready to pounce up my leg with her hands.

I tried to turn my body away from her, but I was seated on White Stripe and couldn't do anything. With my words I said, "I graciously accept your pie but nothing else is necessary!"

"Well, would you mind helping me with a problem inside?" she asked and smiled, "Leaky faucet," ending her statement with a theatrical frown.

I shook her hand off of my leg and sighed as I bunched the reins in my hands. With a touch of my heels, White Stripe and I stamped away down the road. His ears where relaxed, one swiveled towards me and one lackadaisically propped forward. He was listening to me with his left ear as I breathed without assurance, thinking I knew what she had been getting at, but still not knowing. We trotted, then I realized he was relaxed enough for him to gallop as we pushed past acreages of land. I could not see them well, probably because the lens I was using was used to a different reality. I had not asked all of the questions I had needed to ask and answer to live well in the world as I had known it yesterday; what was the probability that I would be able to ask them all here and now, in a world made quite opposite to what I knew?

We began away from the road when I saw a fence knocked down and an obvious deer trail going from it. I kept my hold on the reins loose and as we eased into trots and out of canters, I stopped my old English-riding habit of posting, or bouncing up with control as the horse falls down. We followed that and went past meadows of golden grasses. Next to us, butterflies popped in and out of the ground like dolphins surfing the water. We made progress quickly into a gulch and its ensuing trail into a river.

We followed the trail to a crossing where there were three grizzlies before us. Each of them were apparently hurt, as they were half-lumbering up and half-tumbling down, eyes rolling in their sockets in pain. They moved their large paws like mops, slow moving across the tiles of the water. Unaccustomed to seeing wild animals, I stared wide-eyed. One bear was cyclically raising his head, but like a flag flapping in the wind it would fall, only for him to snap it back up. He whimpered as he gave up the act and his neck stayed at a tight angle, the noises from his throat sounding like baby's coos, bubbly and viscous.

Their groans and moans were entreaties to one another to perhaps assist, but none had the strength of health to do a thing outside of recurrently struggle back up to fall down. The water continued to stream past them catching on their huge forms and splaying out around them. When they fell into it completely, the large bodies of dirty watermelon-colored fish splashed up around them. Their brown coats dripped both water and blood. Each of them looked around dully, lips parted and tongues falling from their mouths as their immense heads turned on their massive shoulders, like incapable children asked to do too much.

I had a moment to gaze from afar as White Stripe had rolled his eyes in the back of his head at the waterway sight and had stamped his hooves to stop. It took some coaxing, but with some eventuality we trotted past the dying trio of beasts. We approached and noticed for the first time that from the water, salmon were snapping and ripping off tufts of the fur the bears had on their bodies.

With overgrown and hooked upper lips, the eldest fish tore at the flesh under the fur and spilled red blood from the grizzlies into the river. Like compact elephant tusks, their large lips clamping and tearing at the bears. The bears were too beaten already to effectively remove themselves. Blood streamed from the necks, legs, stomachs of the bears. As we approached, I began to see more than blood spilling out from the closest one to us. Globules of desaturated pastel colors escaped from a segment of split red flesh under the dark fur. I turned away, yelping, and White Stripe reacted to me, stamping his hooves. I heard the sound of rocks sliding against rocks as he displaced them underfoot and the water chimed in my ears as he splashed, prancing unwillingly further away from the bears, down the waterway, as I tried to reinstate my tight hold on the reins.

I drew my eyes up to the other bank, where I wanted to go, and snapped my heels into his flank but White Stripe began to stamp and snap aggressively at the salmon that had followed tidbits of bear as it slid past his hooves. Now they nibbled and snapped at his legs, as a great white is said to nibble on victims to test it. His ears were against his neck, laid flat as his head raised and he shrieked, a sound like the day might make if taken away from the night for the rest of eternity.

I took the reins in tighter and lifted my legs up off the saddle and back down again with as much force as I could muster. He shrieked at the unexpected peril of my feet on his flanks and rolled his body into a gate that carried us through the water and onto the opposing bank, where I turned him to witness the opposing shore and the tragic ends being met on it, but the stallion under my own petite form had a different idea and pushed us both past the gravelly beach and the heavy forest that ensued. I ducked and, sometimes didn't, appropriately as branches and tall shrubs whipped onto my face and legs. Some tree trunks got so close to my legs that I

47

had to slip them either forward on the saddle or behind it.

This pushed White Stripe hazardously and, realizing he was losing his own control, I talked to him and consoled him, "White Stripe, we're learning that my original assumption was at least close to accurate. Nothing here is as it should be. It is a world of opposites, but if this is how it is, that's how it should be."

He mellowed and allowed me to more smoothly duck and sway as we trotted through the forest.

He snorted loudly.

"What is that, you say?" I asked of him, "You quote Cicero in saying silence is one of the great arts of conversation?" He didn't reply and I laughed jovially at having forced words in his mouth.

He slowed his own pace completely and nodded his neck and head. I was still shaken and only wanted to calm down with him. I let myself shake my arms out, like an upset bird shaking their feathers.

"Pray you now forget and forgive." I told him and added, "That's some Billy Shakespeare for you." I laughed at myself again, only able to sound so silly with a beast and not with other people.

He began trotting again after I remained quieter. He pranced delicately along the wide path and we watched the landscape paint itself.

The view was wide and stretched out to envelop us in it. I looked up at the viridescent sky, trying to grasp an oddity very far from my hands. White Stripe pranced without rest as I led him to an open area for us to relax in. I got off of him, checked maps and the compass, then decided to get back on him and plow our way through the lake valley.

In my hands were the reins and in my feet were the stirrups. At these two points I was connected only, like I was about to take him over a jump and wanted less weight on his back. He surged through the pine, choosing the best path before I even had a chance to see one. I felt faith and trust in him and let him carry me onward until we hit pavement and his stretching canter was hindered to a walk. I patted his shoulder gingerly and swooped my leg over the saddle to walk next to him instead of exhaust him.

Layers of evergreens cascaded into one another, each one a bit more dim and foggy to my eyes. Tiers of trees tore at my eyes, astounding me with the quantity of replication one species could accomplish. The same coney conifer rose from the ones below and beside it, only to give rise to another set of more above it. My eyes made jagged leaps and dips to follow them along as we slowly progressed along the road.

Along the road were the long cones and dried, burnt brown needles that had fallen from the sugar pines above us as we made our way along the narrow raised hilltop road. The smells had changed slightly to those of oil and cut grass. Beginning to show were mailboxes and, behind long drives and nestled in their own clearings, were houses and farms. Orchards lined some, while others were so far from the road, the only trace of them were their addresses, flanking rocks, wood poles, or most-usually, the mailboxes themselves.

The view narrowed and the road widened, only to curve in on itself and back out as it siphoned us off of the ridge we had been on. White Stripe was content to walk along with me and bobbed his head pleasantly next to me. I let the reins stay in my hands softly and he would push his nose gently into my shoulder when he was behind me, like a friend placing their hand on the nape of my neck. When we stopped to enjoy the cascading view, I rubbed the white stripe that ran the length of his face and massaged his chest, where the stripe continued to cut through the auburn color. Feeling him pause, push, and pull with my hands made me sensitive to

49

the places on his skin, muscles, and ligaments that needed my hands' attention. He rolled his shoulders when I held it in my hands and lifted the weight of his body to let me massage deeper muscles. I buried my face in the short and soft hairs of his neck to breathe in the memories his coat inspired: the aroma of a species destined to benefit man.

Of Napoleon, Hegel had said he was history on horseback, but in that statement I saw a fallacy. History was always being made on a horse. History has ridden horses for as many centuries as I could recall. These animals had inspired global strategics and power plays as they were employed. I walked next to White Stripe, a horse of the same caliber as all that had come before him. I felt pride for this limber horse, with ribs bunched like an accordion ready to spring out a song of roaming and war.

We rounded down and dipped into the lower part of the stretch of asphalt we had been plodding along on. The road we were on was perpendicular to another road and we could begin to hear sounds of traffic coming from it as we dipped down and back up once before seeing that the road we were going towards was parallel to the ocean, which twinkled and played in front of us. Boat paths shined and crossed one another in innumerable sets of glimmering, criss-crossing trails. The brilliant waves and rolling arcs of the sea ebbed in to form a cove in the black rock shoreline directly below a giant cliff, where inshore winds met its face and swept past it, onto the grassy knolls and onto the roads that I now sat on.

I was so taken aback by the view, my eyes glazed to stop from taking in my peripherals while I was imprinting it on my memory, that I heard a soft couple of giggles before looking about myself, startled. In between my horse and the two girls sitting in the sun at the T-intersection was only myself. They began talking quickly to me about him as he shied and swung his hips away from me and into the road. I began to calm him and bring him to the shoulder of the road near them as they lifted themselves from their chairs.

"We have a farm stand," a shorter girl with a choppy hair-cut said. "We could feed your horse for you!"

Without prompting, the other girl spoke up, "We have chard, kale, apples..." She trailed off and oggled White Stripe.

"We'd be happy to trade a few pets of your horse if we can feed him!" said the first girl and they both exchanged heavy looks and began smiling together, then at me.

I laughed a little at their generous offer and showed them both of my hands, "I won't stop you, but you have to get him to agree." The shorter girl opened a cooler and White Stripe nickered at the sight of the greens inside. She handed him pieces of dino kale and made to hand one to me.

I declined with my hands and she bit into it herself before saying, "I'm Sasha." I nodded, she looked like a Russian gymnast, wearing a scarf that draped curiously across her body and a heavy, ill-fitting coat. She pointed to her friend, who was creeping towards White Stripe then tucking herself quickly away from him. I got the impression he would not have tolerated her skittishness if he were not being fed so amply by Sasha.

"That's Sabadra," Sasha told me.

I stretched my body, happy to relax it in the sun, both the one above and the one being reflected onto me by the water.

"And you have a farm stand," I stated as I looked it over. Chairs, a painted sign, and a few coolers were the main destinations for my eyes. Scattered at the edges of these things were more objects like books, paints, and brushes. It was a beautiful smattering of creativity and enterprise in a few feet of gravel on the side of a road.

With pride, they both answered, "Yep!"

I couldn't focus my full concentration on the duo while they eased their wary way around the horse they were pushing to spook, so I looked to the white of the sun burning a hole in the emerald silk, draped fabric of sky and the fluttering veil of blue water before us.

Illuminated by more than sun, I saw truths with new light shed on them. The awkward nature of this backwards world was not ever-present. Mechanical rules of the world that I had known were still holding true as I looked at a sun shining on a landscape that I had always known and water moving about the world in the same way. Yes, the colors were slightly changed and oddities existed, but the mechanics were solidly the same, so far.

This could have meant, then, that past knowledge I had picked up throughout life like the sun's gravity and the earth's rotation were not different, but knowledge I could say I and all inherently knew, that the sky is blue, grass is green, and that a bear is scary and big and salmon can be tasty morsels of food for them, were now either flipped on their backsides or anywhere else along a similar spectrum of very different. I could have known even less, now, and I feared that.

I knew my posteriori knowledge, what I had learned throughout life, was intact, but my priori knowledge, the inherent, was shot and gone. I thought of what else was included in that. I sighed and blinked away from the sun.

This was only my immediate reaction, I had to remind myself, and was not all sufficing. What else could be different from what I had known? Not knowing the intricate workings of the planet I was on and all of its systems left a pit of anxiety in my torso as I tried to breathe the heavy sea air in.

One of the girls caught my eye and waved. I put up a hand and smiled to her. I bent over a bit to breathe in and look between my knees. From there, the green sky was a carpet underneath the blue wall of sea and the ceiling of gravel road beneath my feet. I took a breath in and I stood up straight and walked towards the girls. White stripe nickered and I grabbed his reins and gave his nose a pet. Sabadra took a great leap behind Sasha.

"What's his name?" Sasha asked.

I told them, "White Stripe."

"Is that because of his white stripe?" Sabadra asked me as she surveyed the broad line running down his face and chest. I nodded to her and smiled. I tied his reins to a nearby construction truck's welded steel bars and pushed a hand in the saddle-bag to take out oats for him to eat there. There was a dull knife next to them and I took it out to cut the pie. I handed small slices to the girls but only Sasha took one and I ate some, myself.

"What's your name?" Sasha asked me. Sabadra looked to me and shielded her eyes to the sun. I must have been just a silhouette to them.

"Ashna." I told them.

"That isn't a guy name!" Sabadra exclaimed.

Sasha jabbed her in the ribs. "You can't say that about it," she very nearly whispered.

"I was just assuming," Sabadra said quietly.

I told them, "Don't assume that two categories are mutually exclusive or exhaustive."

"Well if there isn't just guys and girls, what is there?" Sasha asked.

"Either you are one or aren't," Sabadra said, clutching her own hands as she nodded with the words.

I smiled at them and turned to start working out rocks in White Stripe's hooves. When I took the pick from the bag I gave my hands a good look-over and saw they were more worse for the wear that I had put them through. I made the decision to wear some gloves as I looked in the saddle bag to see a suede pair nearly resting on the edge for me. I tucked them in my pocket and began hoisting a hoof in between my knees and using leverage to screw a few clods of dirt out of the edge of his hoof's frog.

I smiled and caught myself forgetting to check my chest. I patted it down and realized my predicament. I needed to see if there were more changes.

I turned to the girls and smiled out some words, "I really do have to go take a break with my bladder," they nodded amiably and I un-knotted and pulled on his reins to take him behind the construction truck. I needed to check what was in my pants if there was nothing in my shirt.

An up-ending discovery of both relief and revelation was nestled underneath belt and jeans. The walk-in closet I had been used to had been added to, making a set of drawers I didn't have prior knowledge of. I zipped and buttoned my pants back up.

The girls were sitting back in their chairs, both staring at the landscape and talking to one another at the same time. They had the friendship that was nestled in knowing one another's minds intimately. As they chatted and I rested behind them, I could hear their enthusiastic outbursts and how their statements fluidly finished off the previous moment's words. They were able enough to look at one another's words as they were spoken and see both the historical and the uncreated, but very tangible, thoughts of the girl next to her.

One of them caught me looking over them to the sun and yelled over at me. I led White Stripe over to her, mostly to ask what she had said. Sasha smiled brightly and I felt it must have been a gesture of welcome.

"Hey," she said as a ray of sun poked her eyes, "so what's your story?"

"Haven't got one," I felt the words thick in my mouth.

"We like you, you're welcome to come up to our farm," she shook my hand as she said it and Sabadra wagged her head up and down.

I probably looked as if I was shocked by an electric fence as my hands and feet popped out from where they had been. I smiled and nodded, accepting.

Sasha squealed, which reminded my manhood of its place on my body and purpose, too. I looked to them and asked, "How are you getting home?"

They both shrugged and Sabadra said, "Somebody up there will get us on their way in or out."

The idea of being able to see my reflection in a bathroom mirror, check out the transformation a bit more, and hitch White Stripe up in a barn stall, arena, or whatever they had, was alluring to me. I wanted to follow these girls to their paradisiacal farm.

The need for self-evaluation can become linked with the need to affiliate. The greater the anxiety, the greater the need.

"I don't know if I can do that," I said, kicking the dirt at my feet and watching the waves roll into black rocks below us, "I can't just-"

Sasha laughed and approached me, a finger raised to my lips, "You don't have to be shy, we'll take care of you."

Sabadra made a loud intake of air and Sasha turned to see her guffawing. She hastily added, "Not like that!" She rephrased, "You could use some picking up." I discerned the pair, one voluble and one timid, and saw them as a safe choice.

I nodded, uncharacteristically quiet. I didn't want to make a joke that would confuse them, say a couple of words that would trigger any fear or anger. I stayed quiet to hear what they had to say. Sasha held the reins as I got back in the saddle.

"Go back up the ridge the way you came and take your first right. We live at the end of that dirt road," she looked at Sabadra, who held up numbers as she said, "Our address is 3124 Neptune. Tell them we sent you, or just settle in until somebody chases you out, screaming for you to tell them what you're doing on their property." She put a hand over her mouth and let loose a laugh. I nodded, thanked them both profusely, and twisted the reins in my hand as I got White Stripe trotting up the hill.

Their faces bounced in my mind as I followed their directions, which were simple but arduous as the dirt road was a long one. The way they looked at me and what they felt when they saw me was fresh and somehow new to me. Letting myself be bullied by situations where I had to imagine throwing myself out of moving cars to escape people was antecedent to this experience of being given things I didn't want. It was novel and raw to have been treated well, without apparently hostile allusions to sex.

CHAPTER FIVE

"What did I tell Robert before I took White Stripe?" I asked myself. He raised his ears at the sound of his name, "That I could have anything, but needed nothing. So why is it I don't want what is given to me, now? To be thoughtful and considerate right back to these people offering me things, I need to be able to accept them. I'll go up to this farm and I'll enjoy it, I will."

We both trotted on, me plodding slower in my thoughts than I had ever previously admitted myself to do.

By the time I reached the last driveway, I was symptomatic of my most apathetic self. I sighed at the prettiest tree and laughed when a crow called to me.

"I can't understand," I said as I guided him to turn on the gray dirt, "but I will not falter." What it was that I couldn't understand, had already slipped out of my grasp. I cautiously turned my hand over in front of my eyes. The appearance was new, but not virginal. My skin was weathered and worn in ways and places I had not worked it. It was like I had found a new skin, one that was calloused and covered in all the right places. I felt protected, surrounded by a better defense than I had ever had.

The questioning was still there, a lingering nuisance that asked me to remember the original problem. But was there one? I tried to walk away from it but, like a lead rope I was on, it pulled me back to it. I couldn't face it, but I couldn't leave it.

I sighed at the most beautiful tree and laughed when the crow called.

Swaths of purple bushes pushed away from my eyes and down a bank, leading to an end that I could not see. Each row was made up of spherical bundles of the plant stalks nuzzling to the ground and atop them, their flowers, which pushed to the sky determined to get away. Curving rows close to me were of the most vibrant hues, as the ones that receded in the background were pale and hazy to my eyes. Planned to take over only where they were placed, the lavender was placed like strings of amethyst across the long, soft-sloping hillside, rounding down it and away from my eyes.

I imagined it being more beautiful with more sun, or more wind, or with a different pair of eyes.

A different pair of eyes would see the answer in the beauty.

In a single movement of the world around me, I should be able. Able to see so clearly what I did not know. Without that change of eyes, I would never know what I lacked.

There was movement, though. The wind moved up from the valley and didn't settle until it had run its cold fingers through every plant. Sun burst forth on them and was just as quickly diminished by clouds, which ran the length of sky like it was jade asphalt. There was so much in front of me and I saw nothing.

Rocks tore from the ground to bounce around, hitting metal siding, grass, and fence poles as the truck that brought Sabadra and Sasha home came back to its farm. I looked up with White Stripe, our heads moving together in a simultaneous effort to find out what our future would hold. I looked hurriedly to the horse, like I could find what I needed with him. He raised a hoof and let it push back to earth. I shook my head at us both, like I could find nothing else to question and let the matter go altogether.

I stood where I was while the girls got out, put their signs, chairs, and cooler to the side of the parking shed they were under, then made their way to me.

"I didn't realize just how much you needed to make a farm stand." I put in as they were both closer.

"We didn't realize how-" Sabadra began to say.

"How what?" Sasha asked as she rubbed out teal grass stains on the knees of her jeans.

"Well, it is tiring, being out in the sun and wind with nothing to do."

Sasha looked shocked at her lamentations and, for a moment, seemed like she would remain mute. Sabadra raised her shoulders and hands then let them fall.

Sasha quickly groaned out, "I thought you liked talking to me," she said, "and that we were lucky to get to do that together."

"It feels good to vent or show frustrations," I ventured to say, "I even think that we sometimes say and do those things to hear if they are even true or not as they are coming out."

They had both heard enough and were nodding vaguely as they went to pet the horse, looking like he was ready for the food in the saddlebags.

"Well, we offered for you to come up here, but you have to talk to Bayo."

I raised my brows.

"He owns the farm," they both said. I nodded and they pointed out his house, which was painted the primary colors: cyan, magenta, and yellow. I bid goodbye and asked them to only feed him what was meant for horses and was off. I didn't like finding a source of contention for anyone, let alone strangers.

When I stepped up to the door it swung open to show a woman holding two infants with a third child at her feet. In a distant part of the house I heard the screams of a child and running footsteps of another.

Forcefully entering my field of vision from behind the door was a man, large and of olive-skin tone that shone as he gestured hastily at me. If I had known he was trying to ask me to walk backward, I would not have walked forward into his house. I collided solidly with his chest on my face and my hand on his leg or something close to it. I managed to see the shocked face of the mother as I was forced out of the house.

Bayo grabbed me with his smile, not trying to hide his extravagant need for better workers as he looked over his farm. There were projects missing the hands needed to complete them, and so a few places were tragic mishaps.

He said, as he looked at a house that had been finished then torn back apart, "I tend to see lions come here and see them leave as jellyfish." The easiest way to reason with that seemed to be to watch him as he half-worked rubble out of the wreckage of the house.

He pointed out the old-growth redwood that had been used to make the house.

"Little good that did," I said. He orally explored the ways that old-growth redwood helped a structure while I wondered if he knew what I meant.

At some point, workmen gloves had appeared on Bayo's hands and he was grunting exhaustedly as he lifted with his back and tossed with his knees. I grabbed the riding gloves out of my back pocket and put them on to join in on the effort of strewing materials from one side of the house to another.

It had been built beautifully, letting in light and sunset views- and taken down terribly. It was hard seeing many ways for the damage to be undone. Bayo was full of them, though, as he introduced me to all of his ideas about regenerating his farm and the world at the same time. I got the idea that a productive farm was not enough to him. He thought he would have something he couldn't yet identify, but certainly thought that he needed.

"You can take all of your anger out here, is what I tell most people," Bayo let me know as he groped an axe out of a leather toolkit and began splitting wood quarters. He made a bundle and shoved it into a crook of my arm.

"What if I don't want to do that sort of thing at work?" I asked.

"Get angry?" He asked me, "Any man has some aggression built up. Imbalance in life causes it, and your attitude."

I shrugged, "I don't agree."

"You're a sharp kid, you know."

"I guess I have to agree," I said.

"Don't ever change," he told me, "ever."

I shrugged again.

"My entire life has basically been leading up to this moment," he said as he had me drop the split wood off at his backdoor. We walked away from the house to split more wood.

I thought that both bold and unsure. I said, "How paradoxical."

"I don't know about that," he said.

I looked at him, trusting him less. We moved the long boards out of the dilapidated structure and towards a storage shed for wood.

"How have you seen people turn into jellyfish?" I asked him.

He brushed the question away by asking, "What areas of work are you good at?"

I was forced to answer, "I've always had a good ability at everything," I said, ignorantly, leaving room to imagine a facade of confidence to lean on.

"I have an honest wage for you," he said gruffly.

"I've heard of such things," I replied.

"You're a great worker, I can tell that right off the bat," he complimented.

"I like gardening and keeping up livestock, including my horse, but I don't want to end up mistakenly attributing liking those things to the reward you give me." I thought out.

"I don't think you will," he tilted his chin down as he spoke.

"If you reward people for something, they like it less for what it is and more for what it gives them," I said, as I thought about the way I felt about limiting my love for the things I could do by doing them for money.

He shrugged his shoulders, "You want to be a good worker here. Put your head down, no running around, no shenanigans, nothing."

"Research has shown. Bem, Heider, Festinger, Sherif, et. al."

"I have no idea what you're say-" he stopped himself from saying more.

"Et. al is a fancy way of saying, 'and others' in psych research. The original point is that there's a difference between technical and conceptual problems here. Technically, the money's there and it's good. But conceptually, I don't know. "

He bent his neck to look at me, then smiled and bent it back to look at the cabbage's rootstock, "Crazy. I think you should live here, which is crazy. Right?"

"It is," I agreed.

"Why?"

"The balance theory, alone, justifies my point. I don't like anything anybody else likes. That puts a damper on the balance. I wouldn't mesh."

"Oh yeah?" He looked at me to squint while he spoke through the top two teeth, "Who came up with that one?"

"Heider. He came up with saying you agree with those you like and disagree with those you do not like. If I don't agree with people then-"

He cut me off and said, "Why don't you change? Be flexible. You are a little wet behind the ears."

"You just asked me to never change," I stated.

He looked at me cunningly, raising a finger in the air before letting it fall again. He looked down, and quite suddenly, was laying on the ground, next to a cabbage.

It is a desperate feeling, I thought, understanding that your view of the present is so much different from reality.

"Who keeps sending these up?" He asked, speaking more to the cabbage than to me.

It was that feeling that I tried to hold onto, as well as relinquish. I don't want to crush the idea while trying to hold it in my hand.

"I couldn't tell you. Wait," I said, "aren't you the farmer? You should know how plants grow."

Be close enough to understand but progressive enough to move away from, I thought.

He was still on the ground, "I only grow the Lavocaine. These," he touched the cabbage, "nobody here plants. Something or someone is pushing them up here."

I tried, with fail, to think of reasons or excuses for the cabbage being pushed from the ground by some non-visible being underground, as Bayo must have believed. I couldn't begin to fathom the complex set of reason that did or did not exist behind his thinking.

"Why does Lavocaine exist?" I thought I could try to ask.

Bayo laughed, "Why does anything exist?"

I began, "Essentialist believe things exist because of the essence of that thing was apparent. The need or place in the world existed before it was previously there," I said as he shook the cabbage head, dislodging some of the roots, then continued, "Existentialists think that something exists in a material way, and that their purpose in the world around them develops after."

He scoffed, putting his hands by his armpits, then pushing to stand up, "Existentialists just have a preoccupation with dying."

I cringed, "Existentialism as a feeling means something different to every person." I mustered confidence to say. "These are schools of thought I have studied."

He scoffed, "That doesn't mean they're right."

I laughed and said, "Nor that I am."

"True," he agreed. "To answer your question: Lavocaine exists to be used by man. Everything on this earth is to be used by man."

I laughed, "Man uses whatever is on this earth as he wills, doesn't he?" Bayo nodded, and I threw that argument aside to say, "Poppies are on this earth, but should we use them the way we do?"

He looked at me contemptibly. If I didn't want people to act out and hurt me, I shouldn't act out in ways that hurt them or make them uncomfortable.

"I mean, it's used sometimes for good," I stammered, then reconstructed my words, "But it kills a lot of people."

"That is not the fault of the distributor," he said, no shame in his words or leaking past his teeth.

"Yeah, but if you weren't dealing it in the first pla-"

He cut me off to say, "I'm not a drug dealer."

"I think you are, by definition you are."

"There's a lot of stigma attached to that."

Bayo had a look of indignance pass on his face, an argument forming in his mind, so I began to speak. "What is it, this Lavocaine?" I stuttered, "I don't think we have it where I come from."

"A stimulant and a relaxant, all in one," he said appreciating the familiar sounds as they rolled from his mouth.

"Crazy you haven't heard of it," he said, "given that it is the most widely used drug."

Nothing I knew was going to get me anywhere in this world.

I sighed, "I give up."

He surprised me and said, "I think I like you enough to make you work for me."

"Just because I give up?" I asked, looking up at him.

The time he used to speak was indiscernible and restrained. "Not just because of that, you're smart and I need that here."

I looked up to see a hawk circling wide into the air as crows cawed at it. They fought the wind currents to reach it, but it had more control than them and soared in a hot draft.

"Propositions show the structure of the world, too," I said.

"Well, I'm propositioning you, brother," he said to me. I felt forced into a corner with a nickname and an extended, hopeful handshake. I thought quickly.

I had been controlled with compliments so much before that I started running through reasons he would not try to force me into a sexual relationship. Reasons like his wife and children were important ones and, as a woman, I would create a bond with a man's wife in order to protect myself from any future advances from him. I had also had to remind men of their children when they had come on to me too strongly.

I thought of these simple, but direly important tools before I prompted myself to look down.

I realized I had a flaccid member, which made me as a good as a member of the family to men, now. There would be no unrequited advancements, or at least, less. I smiled to myself before pulling something from my memory to say to Bayo.

"When persuaded or pushed too far, people will react in a way to assert their freedom again," I said quite unassertively, given the assertiveness of the statement.

"What?" He asked, poking the cabbage.

"It's called reactance," I said.

"Well, is it something you see as being a problem here?"

I replied quickly, without thinking, to appease him, "One ushers in what one has a big enough door for."

He tilted his head and squinted heavily, "What does that mean?"

I sighed, trying to explain the inner workings of my mind was not easy, "I only ask for what I can handle. If I've asked for this, I can handle this."

"You quoting someone?" he asked.

"Not at present," I replied tersely.

"I really like you," he said plainly looking at my eyes. "You are strong and smart and, like I said, I need that around here."

I glanced at him and said, "I don't think you understand how much of a problem my self-concept has been having because people are idealizing me based on their indirect or short experiences of me," with reluctance.

He winced at me, pushing his teeth together to say, "Not like that, of course, not as two men."

Knowing I was a man felt good, but hearing from him that I was was something else. I felt pressed. I was not acting it, filling the shoes -body-of man. I was just a woman regretting exploiting something in someone. If they weren't doing it to me was I going to do it to them- or more true might be an assumption that I was the only perpetrator.

While thinking myself a victim while a woman, there was a possibility that I really was hindering other people. If I continued hindering others while a man, I would raise it to a probability.

Man is covered in a soft exterior and a complex interior. I got lost in that interior. I had let my exterior get harder. The hard shell was hard to leave. When you put up walls against others, you create something that you, too, have to climb.

I asked if I liked myself enough to be holed up within it. When there came a person that was enough in love with me to climb the wall, would I force them back over by keeping secrets? There is a difference between being wrong and irrational. Being in love pushed both of these into its equation. There was a difference between being willfully ignorant and being self-deceptive, and while drawing the line between them, I may have been overtly ambiguous.

Questioning my honesty with myself made me also begin to question the person I was quite a bit, stripping away truths until I was looking at small details of myself. Details which told me finite truths. Finite truths that did not lead me to understanding the whole, instead protesting it.

I nearly gave up the act of breathing while getting lost in the labyrinth. If asked to create a facade of confidence now, only a fractal pattern of more ignorance would erupt. It was pertinent to be confident, here, as everyone was out to gain the trust of everyone else. If I had no certainty in myself, I could not trust that they wouldn't be advantageous of that.

A con artist exploits the psyche of an individual by inspiring in them confidence. What was Bayo doing, if not that? To be more open to conflicting facts about my current beleifs was important to finding

I sighed. Bayo smiled. I looked at the colors of fields, farm, and the houses. He smiled. I sighed.

"Want to see where you'll be living?" He asked.

It was out of my character to say, "Why not?"

"Then let me show you!"

I realized that patterns on the farm had already presented themselves. Something was made, it was used slightly, then it was torn down. A fence was put up haphazardly, worked poorly for a month, then left in a state of disrepair or taken apart for materials. Storage was made, used, then left to have rain and wind tear it down. When Bayo showed me the barn it was said that he was going to have a wall knocked down in it. Only in aesthetics was anything wrong with the wall, but he was ready to rip it up.

"Then we'll put a new wall up," he concluded enthusiastically.

Sabadra was painting her nails and looked up, orbs of light reflected out of the dark recess of the barn she was in as she did. They were extinguished from my sight as she looked back down at her fingers, which were far from a light that let me see them.

I asked Bayo, "Are you willing to risk what you've built up for a better design?"

He shook his head, "Well, it-" he started mumbling.

Other people have imposed their desires on you, Ashna, I said to myself, Don't impose anything less than good on them.

Honest thoughts aren't always kind enough to say and so, lying to please others happens. It did make me feel shameful. If my inner thoughts were not adequate for the outer world, my inner thoughts might need to be changed and made better. They were just behaviors, I reminded myself, and not who I was. I didn't have to feel guilty about who I was, just about what I was doing. Feeling better about who I was would probably get me better results when trying to change what I was doing.

"Don't worry," I said to him, "it sounds like a great plan."

He smiled, enthused, "Want to see the drying area for the LC?" He asked, maybe hoping I would

68

validate his plans instead of what was already there, again.

There were no windows, only fans that blew against the hanging lines of lavocaine, its purple flowers and green stalks growing gray as they hung from long lines of twine by twist-ties. I noticed Bayo go to a large, organized pile of black contractor bags and open one by lifting it and lightly pushing the bag until it had untwisted. He gingerly placed it back down and dropped his head to the opening of the contractor bag, inhaling.

"Oh, this is quality stuff," he said, full of pride that he had a right to have.

"You started this business on your own?" I asked.

He looked at me, seemingly perturbed, saying "What?" as he lifted the bag and repeated the process of twisting the top and knotting it. "Of course I did."

As we walked around the top of the barn, I asked, "How many kids do this?" I was worried, but I didn't feel alone.

Bayo opened the collar of his shirt and said, "Kids don't need to be taught not to do drugs," I inhaled sharply and he continued, "we need to teach our drugs not to have anything to do with our kids."

I felt a question was in order and stammered, "What do you mean?"

"We, I mean the technicians in our industry, have been able to extract certain compounds in LC to get at the most potent parts. Along with that, it's completely unusable by children. The compounds that get you high and the compounds that are downers have been extracted from each plant to combine a drug unlike any this world has seen. More powerful or useful than any man-made invention."

"Isn't it man-made if it's been altered like that?" I asked.

"That's not my point," he said.

I asked, "Well, what is your point?"

He continued without hearing my question and I chose to praise him for what I did understand, saying, "We've modified it to get a better hill-"

I cut him off with another question as I mimed a hill. "What?"

He bent over to pick up a few flowers that littered the ground and said, "A hill has an up and a down, like Lavocaine: man's greatest achievement."

Man's greatest achievement. The only thing I had wanted to get away from were men. Man, bulging out of my jeans. Man, somehow pushed into my genes.

I wanted to stop worrying, so I asked Bayo, "You said Lavocaine is what?"

He looked up at me and I thought I saw resentment sweep across his face, "Yes, Lavocaine is a drug and we grow, dry, and trim it., which is all illegal."

"Oh," I squinted at him to let him know I was thinking about it while smiling to let him now I wasn't too confused to hear more.

"That's what worries you but that's also how this is an operational farm. We have chickens, bunnies, and a goat all because we grow it. Those types of things don't make money, they take money. Lavocaine gives us the money. I have professionals that will work with the product. I want you to do the real manly work that won't get done here by those guys."

I nodded my head, feeling berated with the affirmation of my sexual identity being why I got the "manly" work. Would I be able to do the work because I had a man's body or my own strong will, I asked myself, but knew I would only find out after the work and not before."Sounds good," I said, surprised by own detachment from what I said.

"This all requires technological advances and," he let out a breath, shook his head, then breathed in noisily, "I have a feeling that in the future," he was breathing heavy with that fear, "forms of entertainment will be more important than technology. Imagine what will become of a place like that."

"A culture that is as young as ours should not be dictating the way other cultures act. Our culture doesn't have enough experience to be doing that."

He continued, "Follow me. In an ideal world, which none of us have ever lived in, all of these things would already have been done." He pointed to the goat pen, "This is Beatle. We love her." He said it quite plainly. He was very unenthused. "I want her to be pregnant. Well, actually, my wife does."

I nodded, then pointed, "What about this tear in the fence?"

Bayo said they were going to tear down the structure and put up a new one. He showed me where to feed the goat from and how the chickens were fed. He led me around the property naming projects that were half-done or not started. It seemed he met people like me often, very quickly decided they were right for a number of jobs, then they grew disoriented and didn't complete anything.

We stacked firewood into a wheelbarrow together. He began nodding to himself as he made the back-and-forth movement of work. "If we don't put an emphasis on technological advances, we won't have put enough thought into how to properly use them when they come about. We could very well kill our own culture by caring too much about discovering pop culture instead of discovering the sciences and art."

I said, "It make us want to self-destruct our own culture. We can no longer feel shame about our country. No longer feel shame about what we have done but what we can do. If not, we neglect our country's influence on us and others and let it literally take our world down with it."

"It's not the individual's problem, it is society's," he said.

"It's both. That is," I said to him, helping him tarp a pile of wood, "the majority of people, including me, are going through life trying to prove something when really no one has anything to prove or is better than anybody else."

Everyone did have something to offer and the struggle to show other people who I was became something that I thought of as a struggle. It did hinder my ability to communicate with others. The blue of the tarp shone iridescent white where the sun had a chance to hit it. He pointed me to the wheelbarrow and I picked its handles up, pushing forward as he had me follow him to the barn.

"You really think so?" he asked thoughtfully.

"I what?" I asked dazedly.

"Oh, I guess I don't." It was then that I wondered if I was still young, especially in comparison to him. While Bayo had lived more than a quarter of a century, had a family, and it was a possibility that he knew much more than me, I was out of control.

"I don't think I have experienced enough to really say," I told him as my eyes adjusted to the dark of the bar, though sparsely lit my eyes were not accustomed to the sharp contrast it held with the saturation of light outside.

"Experience the world in a different way," Sabadra said from her dark corner. "Experience normalities."

"Like you're doing on a lavocaine farm? Doesn't seem like a normality to me," I said.

"A farm is," she said.

"But are you really farming?"

Bayo signaled to me and we walked out of the barn, "People come in and out of this barn to work here for a quick buck, but you're here for something other than money." He walked towards the twinkling lights of his house.

"Let's think about that," I interrupted.

"You don't need to show off. You're smart, but who do you think you are to be a smart-ass?"

I felt every individual feeling in me mix together to make a mushy soup of anxiety.

He continued, "I have a suggestion that involves a group therapy patient. I can tell you are into learning from others, so remember that this one patient," he paused talking as we approached his door, "was a quiet observer during a hundred therapy sessions until that last one. He spoke up to tell the group how much he had become more capable and confident during that time. Nobody had heard him say a word, but he had learned by listening to theirs. Then he left to get married the next day to the love of his life. Be that quiet observer."

I nodded and he opened his front door. Quickly, a stream of noises came from the inside of house to the porch I stood on. I turned my heels as he went in.

Chapter six

The few weeks after that I grew to know the farm life as a migrant farmer on the West Coast. Feeling the cold fog at four in the morning awaken me led nicely into the light peaking through every drape at seven. I usually put the coops of chickens away in the night to keep them safe from skunks, cats, or coyotes. If I had, I could barely hear the rooster crow in the morning. I wouldn't open my eyes until my legs had swung over the bed and into my shoes. Only then did I know it was time to be awake. I would rub the areas of my eyelids that hurt the most. A good rub of the right part of the socket would upheave any residing stress on the mind. I would open my eyes for a good reminder of where the sleep had set in the pains from the work of the day before.

If there were nice Lavocaine workers around that day, a cup of coffee would be waiting for me when I woke up. Most of the Lavocaine workers stayed only a few days, but everybody learned where the coffee was and made it for everybody else at least once. With that in hand, I was carried by my feet past the goat pen and to the tack and feed room.

The goat got fed first as it would open a hole in the fence if not fed first. If that happened, they would need a farmer there to repair the enclosures that were destroyed. Bayo was no longer a farmer, he was a father, and he spent most of his time caring for his babies, so I was the one that got to do the repairs. I smiled as I passed Bayo's house, full of the sounds of waling from the babies and cooing from the children.

After the goat was fed, chicken feed was spread around and all of the coop doors were opened. I counted them every day to make sure none had died in the coop overnight. There was a dead chicken in a coop when I first got there. I wanted to count the chickens like a baker counts his dozens, hoping for new ones overnight, not less.

I bruised and broke my back purposefully before lunch, so that I could rest over some farm soup, which consisted of mostly eggs and greens. The half hour of pause repaired it and I'd go back to work stronger than before. I would break and heal myself physically, tangibly, and it would feel so much better than being imparted with emotional wounds by others. Sore muscles can be rubbed, but a sore mind or heart cannot be.

I dealt with the dead animals more than anybody else and it began to make me think there was something about them that struck emotion in others when with me there was none. Others avoided the task and I found myself marginalizing the deaths, seeing them as units from which I could move on easily.

Looking at the dead raccoon with no wet parts left, I wondered what part of the forest missed him. A black bag went around this one as I carried it to the green, rectangular, and rusted trash that nobody had put things in, yet. The next day the little boy that lived there asked to explore inside after I had lied to him, telling him it was empty. I lied again to explain why he couldn't go in it. He cried and blamed me for ending the exploration and I grimaced instead of smiled.

I walked past the bunnies and knew that one had pneumonia when I saw it laying in the sun, breathing heavily. Someone else there nodded and said, "On his way out." Later that day, when nobody else was near, I had to put the dead bunny in a shallow grave. A skunk, coyote, or cat dug it up in the night and fluffy fur was strewn about the dirt for me to find. The next day, a deeper grave was made. The day after, another bunny died and its body hardened in my arms. Its body was curved and stiffly set in the curve my arms molded it in. By the time I got to the future grave site, it was stiff enough to hang on the tree branch next to where I dug. It did not take just a few moments to dig it and by the time I was half-finished I thought about professionally digging in the future because of how good I was at it, now. I would visit the graves I dug as often as possible, guiltily wondering if there was anything more I could have done.

When Bayo caught a skunk in a kill trap and handed me a gun, saying, "This isn't a job for a girl," I threw it open, loaded the shell in, aimed, and pulled back. Their gun shot a barrel of liquid fire at the animal, which burst into flames and conflagration as it hit him.

He was right, I thought as I hauled the skunk to the bear trail bordering the farm's property, This isn't a job for anyone.

A jungle is chaos, and so is a good farm. Chaos is creation and destruction. Working on the farm creates and deals with destruction. I pulled plants that were growing too close to one another and placed them farther apart or somewhere else in the garden. I introduced bugs that were likely to fall in love with the garden. I took away ones that were eating their hearts out. Bountiful bushes of berries, ascending apple trees, and rapidly riskier roses got completely pruned back. Where there was nothing, there grew something. Where there was something, there was nothing, then something. But only if I worked hard. A piece of property only is a farm with a farmer.

Bayo would stay inside with his babies and children. He would come outside when new people were introduced and would have me work alongside him after he showed them around. Often, his son would run out and follow along on my duties. His son was a four-year old and brightened my days. I could only work during the day and was the only person that spent time outside, and so was there to watch him play as I worked. He would sometimes ask to go to a part of the farm that would need to be worked on in one way or another by me, and so I listened well when he talked or asked questions, because he was apt to show me just what I needed to see. In the garden his tuft of hair would be even with the tall salad patch around him as he sat and imagined with snails, rocks, roots, and dead stems. His inner experience became the author of the natural world.

The two gray dogs that barked at intruders, tried desperately to sniff the hens, and chased the goats, also protected us all. There were half-eaten apples and bear poop littering the borders of the farm and the dogs kept them back. Some people are afraid of dogs but I'm afraid of a place that doesn't have them. With as many chickens as we had, it was known that there were dozens of varmints that would live to drag them away, but the dogs didn't let them do that.

I said to Bayo that I loved the dogs and he replied quickly, "There is no home without one. That's an old saying, you don't know it?" I shook my head. "No home without dogs, no dogs without homes," he continued

"Is it a true saying?"

"Yep, sure is."

"Well, maybe this is a perfect world."

I tried talking to Sasha while she was there about simple things when her eyes glazed over with the look of someone that had sat looking in the mirror for too long and she twirled a strand of hair in her fingers in a way that looked practiced. I asked about less simple stuff and bought the first round of politeness, but struggled with conversation, and resorted to let my eyes roam drearily around the room as I did. Imposing on others seemed the more likely thing that I did when I had been a girl like her, instead of being imposed on by others. She left within a few days of me arriving, a big stack of cash in her hands, and a broad smile across her face. My perfect world bubble was burst, then.

I got to know the types of people that came through for the Lavocaine industry. They were mostly part of a culture that threw away what they were given after they were done with it. They didn't think about the next step of their own lives and often resorted to blaming Bayo for not paying them enough, housing them properly, or for their own past in a manipulative, vindictive way.

In his defense, Bayo was very busy being a father to his children and couldn't often meet the demands of the child-like adults working for him. They rarely came out of the barn, where they worked on the production aspects of Lavocaine and used it, as well.

This step of the process was technically illegal, as I found out, as the only legal parts of the process were growing it in the ground and using it in the context of medication. Actually getting it ready for medical consumption was strictly legal only in a commercialized and government-sponsored environment.

I heard the guys that helped Bayo grow it talk about the way they only wanted people helping them that were in it to increase the medicinal benefits of the plant, but my poppy to opium argument from the old world I was in made me discount their words almost immediately. They didn't ask me to help them, though, and frequently treated me like I was more of a concern than a benefit.

There were alleviations to my happy isolation, though I never knew if they were gainful or not.

Sabadra came to me and asked what work she could do. The tomato cherries needed stakes put in the ground and ties around their stalks to keep them up. We worked with our heads shaded by the plants and the sun baking our backs one hot day and the next. She joined me again and we weeded the walkways and, with care so as to not touch them and make them shrivel up, around the melon and squash plants. Sabadra voiced her appreciation for the fresh air, sunshine, and sound of birds.

"So much better than being in the barn and taking apart plants," she had said.

"It is better to have someone working next to me." I told her, "Usually I'm just singing and talking to myself. That's a sure route to insanity."

"I read that people that talk to themselves are more sane. Or more creative. They're more something."

"What I should be taking away is that I'm more," I said, an air of pompousness sprouting from my mouth. She replied with a smile and I pulled my hat off to let the sun pull the sweat out of my hair as I continued to bend down, pull up weeds, and toss them on a piece of cardboard.

"I like your long hair," she said to me and I touched it, the ends dry enough to stroke as I smiled.

"Thank you," I said.

"Where are you from?" she asked.

"I grew up in California," I said.

"But, like," she began stammering.

"Polish, on my mom's side," I told her.

"I don't meet very many Polish men," she said.

I tucked my head close to my shoulder and began working as I grunted, "World War Two was hard on us."

"Oh, I'm so sorry."

"Don't worry," I said, thinking about the dozen dead ancestors that had been killed then. "I feel like a rarity, now."

We worked hard for many more minutes before I asked, "If you could say something to anyone right now, what would it be?"

"Anyone?" she asked, pushing her torso up to stand and sighed out, wiping her brow, "I still know the tradition of finding you alone in the den, sitting on pillows and watching The Blues Brothers. I would see you and leave and get dressed in the white button-down and black tie I wore when we first met. We would parallel the scenes, our conversation quelled only when the credits rolled and we would fall into another and stay on the pillows."

She smiled wide, now, her eyes no longer glazed over in reverie, "Awake with one another until the first light came and our shirts glowed blue from the light sky leaking in through our window and I had to leave you for work.

"Before we moved in together and before we knew how to fall into one another, you met my family and my dog. When you met him, he put his paws on your hips and you scratched his head and I saw the love you had for others. You asked what his name was I said, 'Abel,' searching for recognition and appreciation in your eyes. You told me not to get another named Caine. I laughed and your eyes shown and that memory melds into the one from the canyon and I remember the trust you had in Abel when we stumbled across the rattlesnake there and how you let him find us a new trail, when there appeared to be only one and from then on I knew I could trust you with all things, in every way. That's what I would say if I could say anything to someone right now."

"That was lovely to hear," I said over to her, as she stooped down to tear a particularly difficult and bulbous branching weed out of the ground.

"It was lovely to be asked," she said, resuming her work, for she had stood at full attention as she spoke. Perhaps she was seeing her feelings splashed across her horizon or deeply drawn across her vision in order to witness them.

"Should I ask who you would say that to?" I asked.

She giggled and put a hand over her mouth, "No, you shouldn't."

"Okay, okay."

"I heard there would be rain tomorrow," she told me.

"Well, then we need to prevent the tomatoes from going to rot. We have to cover them from the cold with some burlap or plastic. Do you know where that is?"

She nodded and ran off, then returned with bundles of transparent plastic sheets, "They use this for the Lavocaine drying," she told me.

"Strange business that is," I said, taking the bundles and punching stakes through it.

"Why do you say that?" she asked, mimicking the way I was working the plastic.

"Our bodies have drugs in them already." I said, "Chemicals that our body makes to be happier or more energized or mellow. Why do we need external drugs?"

"Some people's chemical makeup means that they don't get the right amount at the same time or it doesn't release or something, so they take the drugs and it helps."

"Do you?"

"Yes, I do. I use Lavocaine a lot, actually."

"Oh." I staked the first pole into the ground and spread the plastic, listening to the *wahoopawoop* sound it made instead of creating more words, which perturbed me, instead of eliciting joy.

The next day the sky was thin and expansive in the morning. The clouds looked trapped in the farthest layer of sky, pushed away from the storm's mass as it entered. Unsettling every branch, bush, and grass, a deep wind pushed its way over the land

and pulled its way out moments before I felt warm pricks of rain.

Water dropped like pearls from worked and weathered hands of the cobalt and azure leaves, undulating outward from where the water collected next to the stems. Droplets formed tentatively, seemingly never ready to rush down the valleys embedded in the leaves and petals. They would halt and stop before running down the capillary-like wrinkles of the leaves. Tinier droplets would rush down the veins of the leaves at the last moment and the droplets would bulge and swirl. When they did, it was at the moment when they piqued in size, at which point they looked like opalescent pearl forms, dangling from the ears of the leaves, before leaving them.

I was in the garden when the rain started and left it after I had hidden some tender plants under tarps. I was surprised to see the crew that was usually doing work in the barn helping Bayo on the top of his home.

From the roof, one of them yelled, "I need it tied down over here!"

"What's going on?" I yelled to them.

"We're tarping up," yelled Bayo to me as he struggled with the plastic, "areas of the roof," a gust of wind and rain pushed him around before he finished saying, "that can set fire. We don't get too many of these rain storms a year, but when we do, it can get bad."

"What?" I vociferated up to them. "That doesn't make any sense, it's raining." As I said it, I remembered all of the crazy things that had happened to me. One of the workers began to raise his hands up and made eye contact with me, about to explain, but I threw my words out quickly, "You know what, nevermind it! Good luck," and I walked away.

I heard some shrieks when I was tending to White Stripe and I looked in the direction of Bayo's house to see small flames. I ran out to see that they had been extinguished by the time I was close enough to actually gauge the situation. I shook my head again, mystified, before a revelation struck.

I asked, "Is White Stripe in a dangerous area?"

Bayo yelled, "Inside the animal's barn is very safe, dry. Not a good place for the fires to start."

"All righty, that's weird, but all right."

I ran back to the paddock where White Stripe was, yelling to him as I opened the gate, "Bad weather, huh?"

He was looking melancholic as the sheets of water began teeming about his back and withers, stringing on him like a corpse infested with insect trails. I held my hand out and he didn't move, staying shocked to his position.

Wiping layers of waterlogged hair off of my face, I sighed, and chose not to grow resolute with him, but became proactive. I grabbed his halter from the hook on the gatepost and put it over him, tying the lead rope to the metal square near his lip on one side of his face and latching the clip onto the other. With that in hand, I led him to the fence and used it as a way to get up on him. My rump was immediately soaked from sitting on him, but while we walked out of the grounds of the farm, I felt us both warm a bit. I knew we didn't want to be out too long, just long enough to warm him up, and started him at a trot as we followed the ambling bear trails from the farm into the dense surrounding redwood forests. The damp made the usually pale bark a deep mahogany and the same change in hue could be said for the jutting pine needles as they fanned out above and around us.

We happened upon the chance open space in the forest. It was a clearing with stubbles of blue grass raising from the ground, encircled immaculately by redwoods growing hundreds of feet up. Every branch was layered so that they were all succinctly able to soak up the sun's rays when it was out, but now as raindrops fell it looked more like we were standing in the eye of a hurricane. All of the trees had spiraled up in just a way so that their branches patterned out to make an intricate network that could have passed for an illusion of the eye. Water flew down at us in the great spiral pattern the grove instilled on the wind draft. It was an exquisite sight to my sore eyes. I was enthralled and suckled on the teat of allowing myself to be mesmerized and enchanted for too long before I reasoned that we should continue on.

I pushed him into a trot from the glade and we took a new trail of our rambunctious following. As was likely, we came upon a fallen log, scratched by bears for worms and insects, the detail of which I was only able to see as I pushed White Stripe to jump over it. Normally when a horse is jumped, the rider's body is making contact with the horse at two points: the feet and hands. I thought quickly, wondering what it would be like to jump him, for the first time, and without wearing a saddle. My muscle memory forced out my analytics and I did nothing differently, holding a form that took my weight off of him as much as possible, pushing on the meeting of his back and neck with my hands and pressing my heels down and into his flanks. He executed the jump perfectly and I worriedly saw our landing had another, smaller, fallen log barring the path. He landed with his front two hooves and, noticing the second obstacle, brought his back hooves to the same place and raised his front hooves up, quickly clearing it.

I whistled and shouted a few moments after my breath had been caught, "Well done, boy! Let's make our way back, now." I turned him right towards a trail, finding a muddy one that should have led us back home.

We pounded along it until I slowed him and realized we had a dip in the trail to traverse. I thought to stop him and look at the best way down it, but the pressure of slowing had made him lose traction. Like a car that has lost power steering on an icy road, he was moving rapidly down. He was not lifting his hooves, but remained steady and exerted pressure against the ground as the rolling, boiling mud below us pushed us forward. There was little time to act, and even less time to think about what to do to alleviate the consequences of the situation.

I raised myself into the two-point position again, taking my weight off of him for mobility on his part and to let him know what I was also telling him with my words, "I'm ready to jump." With the force of the slipping mud, we were dispatched down the hill quickly, turning with it and sliding into the waterlogged apex of the corner as he regained composure and footing. Without warning, he was digging his hooves into the mud ferociously, making up for lost control by cantering up the hill opposite the one we had descended down. I saw his head shake as he gnashed past discomfort and pushed on.

"Woh, boy," I said when we had crested and were looking at the rain-swept Lavocaine fields. All of the bushes had been cut of their purple foliage and there were bulbous masses, perfectly sculpted into spheres, dotting the long stretch of land.

We walked slowly towards them and, as I had always wanted to race through the line of grapes where wine was raised, I found my opportunity to do the equivalent of that here.

"Hiya!" I yelled as I spurred him into a gallop across the line we had chosen. The mud tore past my eyes and gripped onto my torso and thighs as we plowed the ground and pushed far from the discomfort of the ride. I slowed him to a walk and got off as we walked nonchalantly through the farm area.

A man was insisting on tearing apart from the group of Lavocaine workers and coming towards me, yelling, "You got a problem?"

Instinctively, I held the lead rope further from him and walked between him and White Stripe, saying, "I don't think so, do you?" I saw Sabadra move away from her compatriots and approach me. She held out a hand and looked to my horse. I nodded to her and handed her the lead rope, watching her shuffle ten yards away with him.

The man tore his shirt from his body and threw it down, "We worked hard on those fields to protect them from mold these past few hours and you just go through them like you don't even care! You've got a problem!"

"Do you bite your thumb at me?"

He asked, "What was that?"

"Do you bite your thumb at me, sir?"

"Are you trying to get out of this fight?"

"Do you quarrel with me?" I voiced.

Shaking his hands above his head, he asked me, "What did you say? "

I said, "Are you picking a fight?"

"Yes!" He threw his hands down, drawing my eyes to the muck on the ground and the apparel of his that lay in it, getting an idea of my own.

"So be it," I said, smiling, and picked up his shirt from the mud. I held it in a hand as I took off my own stained and muddy shirt. It felt freeing to be able to disrobe in front of others, an opportunity that had never presented itself to me, as a girl, and I appreciated the fleeting moment during which I could feel the biting wet rain pricking against my exposed chest. I did not halt, though, and I put on his shirt, which happened to have some intricate white gothic designs over the black of the fabric. I handed him mine, assuring him with a smile.

His eyes reeled and I saw the sinister sneer vanish from his mouth as his eyebrows hit one another in perplexation.

He asked, "Did you just put on my shirt?"

"Yes, I did. Now, do you bite your thumb at me?"

"No."

"Do you bite your thumb?"

He looked around, at the few spectators, the rainy farm scene, then at me, "No, I don't."

"Good. I'll be on my way, then. Sabadra," she handed me back the rope holding White Stripe. "Thank you," I said, willing my body to relax and for White Stripe to follow suit. He was haughty and stamped aggressively about the barn after I had tied him up inside.

"Mellow out," I told him, "I need to wipe all of this mud and rain off of you. It might help if I took off this joyful man's shirt. Pretty smooth moves on my part out there, eh? Oh, White Stripe, it's things like that...."

Days passed and I felt a loneliness that was a comfort wash over me, as it had in the past and as I hoped it would in the future.

I immediately felt like I had tarnished my image by being too embarrassed to have an image in the first place. The people that were attracted to helping with Lavocaine had their own self-concepts focused around ecology, sustainability, and the like. I let on that I was like them by not saying anything about my interests or dis-reputing theirs. I was trying to minimize who I was when I tried to quietly observe. I felt more needed when I let people know just how much I knew. I felt more like we helped one another.

When Sabadra stopped working with me that second day, I hoped that it wasn't because of one of the many things I had or had not said. When I realized that we both didn't like talking to one another, I blamed myself, mostly, for being so dull and boring to her. Bayo came up to me after bringing in a new goat, he mentioned he had problems with the Lavocaine workers taking any time off.

"What do you mean?" I asked, worriedly.

"They should keep their heads down and work," he said.

"Aren't you paying them per pound?"

He looked at me skeptically, "Yes. But they should still be working from sun up to midnight. No reason for them to be doing anything but working."

I calculated and asked, "What do you call what I'm doing, then?"

He shrugged, "Well, you are farming. That is work, but it's not the same kind of paid work. Do you understand?"

"No."

"I don't get money from what you do, but I get lots of money from them doing what they're doing, so I want them to do it as much as they can."

"I don't like knowing that my friends are working in these awful conditions."

He looked aggressively at me, "Check your privilege at the gate, kid, when you're on my farm you are under my rules. Plus, she and everybody else in there have chosen this life for themselves."

"And what life is that?"

"One where they and I make lots of money," he said.

I judged the situation, thinking of the poor living conditions and the poor working conditions, feeling deeply for anyone that chose to do that kind of work.

"It is better than working behind a register or a desk all day, is it not?"

I was at a loss for words.

"Is it not?" he asked again, laughing now.

"I don't know why I even need to be here."

He said, "If you were not, the entire land would run amuck. I would have to get out there and do the work."

"But you have underground creatures that plant things," I pointed out.

"Above ground there are problems, though," he said, "that you fix very well."

I sighed, "I'm hearing some things from you that I didn't want to ever hear, like saying they should just keep their heads down and work is a terrible thing to say. I don't want to hear things like that about people I know, or anyone else for that matter."

He twisted his face and ran his mouth until his words had finished falling out, "If a tree falls in a forest and nobody is around to hear, does it make a sound?"

"That's a rare occurrence" I spat back, "because, technically, all forests have animal life, and the majority of animals have some sort of auditory capability."

"Huh."

"Re-think your goals and how you're warping other people."

"Most of these people don't know where they're going next," he said. "They are in a transient mindset and I'm not taking advantage of that, I'm giving them work. I'm giving them hope."

"Uh-huh." I felt closed and done with him talking my concerns out of me, only to push them aside.

His tone was ingrained with graciousness, "I am indebted to you, in a big way."

I scoffed, "Why?"

"You have done some very wonderful things here."

"Thank you, but I don't know if it deserves me doing things here, anymore."

"The land?"

I shook my head, looking at where the tree's tops met the sky, "No, the people on it."

He stalked away and I played at alleviating the stress of the conversation with other thoughts. I walked on the premises, over to the apple orchard. The apples were dropping freely, fumbling their way past branches and finding their way to the ground. When they didn't get picked off the tree or from the ground, they turned to rot. I had been told they severely interfered with the Lavocaine and that they needed to be removed daily, but hadn't done it once. Perhaps it was an inconspicuous act of defiance. Perhaps I was truly lazy underneath it all.

That afternoon, I picked an apple up, turning it over in my hands. I bit into it, letting the juice crush under my teeth and foam out the side in a trickle. Without taking another bite, I threw it without any cogent path. The tall, wooden, gate surrounding White Stripe's paddock intervened and it landed against the top of it with a soft impetus before falling to the ground beside it. I heard White Stripe's nicker and the sonorous sounds of his feet, but couldn't see him. His breathing became full and minatory as his lips pushed against the wood-grain separating him from the fruit.

I picked up another and swung my arm back and forward, releasing it and watching it fly sharply to the left and hit dirt far before it could hit the fence. I hurried around, setting up a pile of apples and then stood next to them, adjusted my stance, and picked up a third apple to throw. It sailed across the sky, finally clipping the gate and rolling in the air. I heard White Stripe nicker contentedly a few moments after it had fallen.

I picked up another, smiling, and projected it further into his arena. I let loose a volley of three and I could hear his hooves press against the ground as he ran from one to the other. I tried to place his body and throw close to him, realizing the fault in that only when I heard a shrill whinny after a resonant slap of an apple, supposedly against his body. I imagined the way the dust would bloom from the place it had hit him and how, unwillingly but out of force of habit, he would turn and stomp towards the apple, to eat it. I walked the short distance between the apple trees and his paddock, slipping to the left to go in through the gate. He pranced about, nose flared as he sniffed the ground for more of what I had been giving him.

"No, no," I said, "too much of them will give your hooves reason to rot. Too much of anything will make you sick."

When a young girl came to the farm to see about riding White Stripe, I asked her to ride him around in the smaller, circular ring. She knew her brushes as we got him ready and she knew how to tack him up quite well. I was surprised when she had trouble getting the bridle on him. He reacted by sidestepping and raising his hooves, stamping aggressively against the ground with his front foot. She had moved his halter from around his face to around his neck while she prepped to put the bridle on, but he thrashed his neck and the rope that connected to the posts on either side loosened, then tightened as he swayed his head.

She persevered and her hands fumbled at putting the bit in and I jumped calmly forward, looking White Stripe dead in the eyes and saying, "Woh, pony." My body was between the two of them and I was slowly pushing her backwards with my hand behind me.

"You okay, now?" I asked him. I had seen the mustang in him come out, the unruly nature overriding the normally calm demeanor.

"Shhh," she said to him, stepping aside and putting a hand on his shoulder.

I gave a laugh, more to calm him and her than to tell a joke I had heard, "Why do people say *shhh* to animals? They've never said anything."

"That was funny," she laughed and I saw the young, developing teeth in the back of her mouth. I smiled down at her, nodding.

"Why did he do that?" she asked me.

"Horses are like really intelligent cats. Do you know that cats don't like changes? They don't like it when you move houses or switch up a routine. Well horses can be like that. They want things, especially things that can hurt like the bridle or bit of the bridle being put on, to be done the same way. Here, let me show you," I stood behind her as I placed her hand on the top of the bridle that sat under the forelock of hair that fell between his ears. "Now, here," I showed her how to hold onto the bit piece near the bottom of the bridle with four of her fingers and to leave her thumb jutting out. "Now, push against the very back of his mouth with your thumb, it opens his jaw up like that," she slid her thumb past his closed lips and I said, "and now wiggle it around." His lips made a suction cup noise as they opened. "Slip it in all the way and put the top piece in place at the same time," I told her. She did and the bridle was in place. "Good."

She looked up at me smiling, "I don't do that part a lot."

"I can tell, but you learned, didn't you?"

"I did," she smiled.

"Horses are very good with words. Researchers say they are able to learn more than dogs, so I want you to start saying things to him that you'll say in the ring."

"What kind of things?"

"Things to calm him and things to let him know he did what you wanted," I offered.

"Pretty prince."

"That's good," I said, leaning back on one of the poles he was tied between.

We adjusted the stirrups, putting her hand against the saddle and having the stirrups go only where her armpit was. I put a child's helmet on her and she got on him. I stood in the center of the ring with him on a long lead that I held, watching them ride the circle at a slow trot.

"Ask him to canter," I said loudly to her as I realized she was doing well.

She nodded curtly and clicked her tongue as she tapped him with her heels.

His front hooves jutted out quickly and for a moment, I thought he was preparing to rear, but he was stretching his legs before pounding the dirt with them. He kept up a consistent canter. His ears swiveled back to listen to her as she clicked her tongue and gave directions to him. I heard her call him a "pretty prince" and chuckled, noticing that he was receptive to the monicker.

Her seat was not steady and my eyes followed along her body until I saw the problem and said: "Heels down." She nodded again and pushed her heels back down. I didn't know if she knew, so I gave her a tip, "If your toes are pointed down instead of your heels and he trips or something, anything, you would go flying out of the saddle. Plus, you want to keep pressure on him with your heels or he'll start to control you." She squeezed her calves against his side and I could see the muscles in her thigh tighten against the saddle as she did, "Very good, that's it. Now, tighten up your reins. Very nice."

Bayo came out to watch. "A little young to be wearing those shorts, isn't she?" He asked as the sun hit his eyes, bringing out the gold in the brown.

"If she's too young for them, then she is too young to be sexualized in them," I said.

He squinted at the pink fabric bunched above her legs, "You said it. She's ruining her own innocence by wearing those."

I said, "Sex and embracing your sexuality does not destroy innocence, Bayo."

He looked at me and chuckled, "You think?"

"Yes," I said, "I do. I think you're very wrong."

He chewed his knuckle as he watched her in the ring, "She should be more afraid to wear things like those. See the words across her butt? She should be worried about people staring at her backside all day."

"So innocence can only exist in tandem with fear?" I said.

He stared and said, "She's acting easy."

"Girls don't have levels like you're playing some game with them. They aren't easy and difficult. You aren't winning anything by getting so-called easy girls or girls that don't want to sleep with you, either. It's just- oh, it makes me so mad I can't talk straight."

"Watch it, I have a wife," he said.

"I know you do, that's why I'm so worried for you," I vehemently replied.

"Hey, now," he warned with a growl before letting his eyes roam back to her as she was thrust up and down in the canter.

"You know, I like a few things," I began, "I like Ramen noodles. I like hot dogs. I like bus rides. I like all of those things and, guess what they are for me," I said. "As you should know, they're inferior goods. As your ability to have them increases, your desire for them decreases. It's usually applied to economics, but I don't think you should apply it to women. Or," I looked down, "your pants. If you can't have it, don't desire it." I told him, then yelled to her as she looped around the ring, "Bring him back to a trot, that's it." I turned to him, "I'm tired of being that quiet observer," I stated at Bayo as I ground my teeth at his eyes that were trained on the girl.

"What's that?" he asked me without looking at me.

I watched the two riding for a long time, thinking about him and what he was doing. I watched them until I saw White Stripe's ears turn back when she was not giving directions and pull on the reins, nearly taking them out of her hands.

"Ho, pony," I yelled across the ring.

He tugged against the reins lighter, then his ears swiveled towards me, then forward. I knew a ride was more nejoyable when the horse was relaxed and saw her seat become more frantic, less controlled, atop him.

"I'm leaving," I said, a distaste in my mouth.

"What's that?" he asked again, but looking at me this time. I yawned wide, a tactic to de-stress our conversation and get White Stripe to see I had no concerns and that he shouldn't, either.

"Let's go for a trail walk," I yelled to the girl as I opened the ring door.

"Alright!" she yelled back. She brought one side of the reins towards us and trotted him past us, nodding slightly to Bayo as she did.

"I need to sleep on it, but don't expect me around tomorrow." I was speaking more to myself than him. I had a decision to make about staying there any longer.

That night I wished for sleep to take me quickly and the next morning I woke hoping for night's return. Waking only to want to fall asleep was hard on me that once; I didn't ever want to make a habit of it. So, I packed the saddlebags that had been nestled under my bed and hugged the Lavocaine workers that were there. White Stripe's ears pushed towards me as I approached with them and he walked towards me, nibbling on my jacket until he found my hand on his nose. He lifted his lip and found my fingers, closing his lips around them. I smiled, knowing full well that he was leaving a viscous combination of chewed grass and saliva on my fingers, but I let him continue his grooming of me before I led him to a place to tack up and get on.

Leaving felt synonymous with failing. Leaving was only wonderful until somebody wanted to do it to you. I quit thinking. I let my mind and eyes think staring at clods of dirt on the trail was more important than having my thoughts make my grip on myself seem slippery.

When people say, "Stay. All you have to do is be you, stay," how do you tell them that you can't be yourself around them? The argument they would provide was validation enough that they weren't there for me. Every time I did something that I shouldn't be doing, like leaving, I wondered if it would make it that much easier for me to do it again and again, until I didn't notice I was doing it anymore. I didn't want to train myself to do the wrong thing over time by continuing to do it every time.

CHAPTER SEVEN

It was early enough that it was still dark and I blew out into the darkness. From my body came my breath, so hot that I could see the steam. I watched the swirling clusters of steam churn into a vibrant color display. Immediately, I scrutinized it, for it was no standard vapor billowing forth from my lungs but a spectrum of color moving in the air before me.

I blew smoke-o's and tried to french inhale my own miasma, but the wind slowly blew the hot, moist, rainbow-colored air away before I could re-inhale.

It was odd, in the way that paleontologists testing bones with their tongues is odd because bone is porous and your tongue would stick to it. In the way that if you're standing on a very large flat surface and you look up, you'll see what looks like the earth enclosing around you, only because light will curve back on itself, given enough time and distance. It was unexpected, like the way that the brightest things in the cosmos, quasars and blazars, are caused by blackholes, the darkest things in our cosmos. It was odd because it shouldn't make sense, but there it was, making sense by simply existing.

A small puff of steam escaped my nose and I watched it churn out in a rainbow swath of steam in front of me. Expansion happens much faster than light travels, I thought as I let a ring of smoke bounce off my throat and into the cold of the coming morning. It glittered blue, green, yellow, and red as it receded away.

I looked at my forearms, drawing them away from the leather of the saddle and bridle. They were stiff and segmented, stronger than they had been before I hardened them with work at the farm, but were still the length of body that I had known before. Freckles flowered in the same places and when I twisted it, the same gulleys were there. I had not changed too much, and the ways I had were barely apparent. My ruddy blonde hair was no longer long, but cropped close to my ears, bangs shaking out in front of eyes, at times. My hips were slimmer, legs skinnier, and my torso was lean and longer, as well.

The world around me had become an opposite of sorts, but it was not a better place for it. Wishing for the perfect world was no way to get it. I sighed out and watched the color steam from my body, transient reds were churning into the yellows and greens until it evaporated into the air.

When I had become so opposed to the charity that men thought they were giving me, I opposed it. When I had been both comforted and cajoled by men for being a woman with statements like, "It must be easy for you because you're a woman," and, "be careful, you're a woman," I had seen them as thinly veiled stereotypes and opposed them.

Men kept up stereotypes about women always talking when men will never stop talking, like a dog at an endless bowl of food. Men had laughed at the way women went out in groups then chastised them when they were taken advantage of alone.

I was told that to avoid being raped and abused, I should begin acting different ways. Men had told me how to behave so that I didn't get hurt by them. Me avoiding the possibilities just left other women that were walking alone, in the dark, wearing the wrong clothes, that much more exposed. Men assumed women were insecure wrecks that constantly need to be told that they are really beautiful princesses. Women would not be in need of ego-boosts if they were not excluded from a dominating social class.

It was a lot like telling them to continue to be oppressed, actually. Men telling women how to be controlled is a lot like white people telling minorities and, especially, black people how to be controlled. It does not benefit the oppressed group to let the oppressor keep talking. They'll just take them through a system of inequality when they do.

Here I was, I groaned, with a lonely cock in a world where I feared the control of the cock. Here I was, I groaned, making the best of it because life is superior at showing off its creativity. To make myself laugh, I noticed the similarities in the way spontaneous and inexplicable arousal appeared in a moment as a man, to the point where I would tuck my head down to look at it and think, "Hey boy, what'd you see? What is it?" There wasn't much else I could do about it but try to shove it between my legs, so I laughed them off.

As a girl, I didn't know if I was horny, bored, hungry, or tired. There would be a tingling feeling a lot like getting into a hot tub or a great trembling, like my cervix was a golden retriever shaking wallpaper glue off of itself.

It was the only funny thing my mind could bring up as the solitude of a breaking dawn exploded on the road ahead. We passed where I had met Sasha and Sabadra and White Stripe dropped his head to puff his nostrils on the ground where the stand had been. The construction truck where I had tied him while I peed was still in the turnout. I couldn't stop thinking about the farm, realizing humans are hardwired to think everything is interconnected, but that that wasn't the case. Or didn't need to be the case. The things that the drivers had said while I was hitchhiking didn't need to have a place in my life, but I internalized them. The things that the Lavocaine farm had shown me didn't need to have a place in my life and I didn't need to internalize them. But I was. It was over, I told myself, forcing contentedness to spread throughout my body.

I smiled as I looked down with him and flailed my arms as I looked up. There were three puddles fifty yards ahead of us in the turnout. Of them, one was fully ablaze, a flame as tall as me and a few feet around, and the other two had sparks and crackling bits of flame of varying sizes launching upwards. I was preparing to curse in fear as White Stripe felt my intake of breathe. Before I could ask him to, he was turning without being told. I saw the white of one of his eyes and the shaking forelock above it as his neck bulged in flight. I gave slack on the reins and he was able to hurtle up the hill we had come from.

Anticipating his climb up the hill gaining momentum, I cautiously looked back. I could see only one puddle, the smaller of the three, sitting idly with mild sparks just close enough to ripple its surface. The blue of the water from the puddle was distinctly water in contrast the hot red of the flame. I tried to look into its depth to see what was causing the ignition, but we had moved away too quickly. The other two puddles were consumed with flame, almost masking the water underneath them and becoming less than discernible puddles.

White Stripe's hooves clapped against the hill and I felt his backside propel us up it. I worried about going past the first road on the right, afraid Bayo or someone from the farm would be driving down it. The tingle of fear down my spine made me nervous. The prospect of second goodbyes was even worse. I realized that we were going back the way we had come and slowed White Stripe, pulling first on both reins then only one.

He turned hesitantly with that single pull and I guided him back down the hill. I knew that both of our eyes would flicker to the fiery puddles and so I gave a great big yawn, held the reins confidently, and sat straight and strong in the saddle. It relaxed both of us. A lick of flame detaching and momentarily living freely above the rest scared us both, but I yawned again before his body could shake too much to scare and we managed to get to the bisecting road. I turned him left and we started south.

Few cars were on the road so early, but when they did come upon us to pass, they would make White Stripe's ears flicker behind him. I noticed his knees wavered at the blaring sound. His eyes would turn with his head to register where the sounds came from, their sometimes piercing rumbles petitioning his attention.

To calm him, I would yawn extravagantly and as I did so, he calmed. I showed him that his fears were unjust while I yawned loudly, my seat pushing relaxedly into the saddle as I lifted my arms and gave my soft sound of relief. His gait changed, he was less tense, more calm and the school bus that was behind us flew past, his pace tranquil while it did. I tapped his shoulder with my gloved hand, feeling it more synthetic than if my bare hand was rubbing his hair down. He did not shudder again as it was directly next to us and its sound faded quickly, like an approaching ambulance, or a star burning brightly as it approached the viewer, us on Earth, then faded as it grew further away.

There were few other cars, though, none for the first hour we rode and it was with a trot that we made our way on the road skirting the ocean. It must have been the 101 Highway that we were on and I knew we would have to get off of it when there was more traffic. The road winded around and slipped perilously close to cliffs.

"The moon is silly," I told the horse, when the moon wasn't visible, "For following the Earth when the Earth is just following the sun."

Light seeped from the East and the sun peeled away a layer of indigo clothe that the early dawn had worn as a dress for saying goodbye to the moon in. I watched the moon, brilliant at dawn, fade into the bright light of the pastel sky.

"I missed talking to you. You know this is one thing that wasn't so great about staying at that farm. We'll talk more, now. We'll talk, now." He stopped and I pushed my heels in, but he began pooping and I shrugged, "Good artists draw contradictions to show the limit of truth." He moved steadily below me and I perused my head, finally saying, "Contradictions also support beliefs. So, if everything in this world is a contradiction, my beliefs must change with this new world and its new information. But I still don't support Lavocaine after being on that farm. In the world I just came from people say, 'God put it on this earth so we should use it,' to something less harmless than heroine, but they forget poppies were put on this earth and we probably should just not even go there. So, that's absurd. Just because something exists, we shouldn't use it. But see, that there is a contradiction, me saying we shouldn't use everything means I need to have a look at what it is I use and whether I should be." I sighed heavily.

When three or four cars zipped past us, I decided to not get back on the road, but crossed it. We pushed up a deer trail and went a little inland until I realized we were on an open stretch of untamed land. I turned in the saddle to un-cinch the saddlebags from their moorings on the saddle and slung them over my left shoulder. I lifted my leg and tightened the girth, then put it back down and held both sides of the reins with my right hand, tugging them a few times upward to let him know I still had control, even with one hand.

I put most of my weight on my right thigh and lifted my left side. With my heel, I kicked into White Stripe's ribs, then held my foot there for a heartbeat before letting the strength move up into my shin and knee. My left foot remained planted and he used his left leg to push off the ground, first. It gave him a burst of energy for his right hoof to hurtle forward, finally finding a place in the ground a foot or two from where it had been. It dug in as his back legs sprung up to his waist and pushed back down. It sprung quickly, then all but one of his hooves was airborne. His weight and mine shifted from only one or two hooves at a time, leaving us completely airborne for a fraction of a second and a multiple of a moment. It preceded his inevitable push from one side or the other, back or front legs ricocheting from the ground, then back up to his waist or shoulders.

During the gallop, there are too many ways to fall. As you ride the first few times, you think about what to do if a hoof gets caught in a hole, a muscle pulls, something falls out of the sky in our path, and how to deal with those things. After a while, the reflexes and muscle memory do the thinking for you, pulling you and pushing you to stay balanced, ensuring an unperturbed ride, and in case of any bad happenstance you have the reflexes from fear built up to protect you.

It reminded me of running meditation when the road was safe and you didn't have to consciously think about your step. There are no hazards on the ground and you could begin to take steps without thinking, without consciously shifting your weight back and forth. It was something happening very far away that you didn't need to be a part of, all you had to do was have the will for it to continue.

I slowed him to a trot after a good stretch, worked his shoulders with a few pats, shifted the saddlebags, and tried to pass a few minutes by at the slower pace before starting a gallop again. His hooves pushed away dirt and grime from the ground and into the air, sometimes onto me. The outside of my shins became caked in clods of red mud and white dust. My fingers couldn't move outside of the position of the reins, and my legs, of course, became bow-legged when I got off of him to walk or rest. We rode on, though, intent on escaping the loneliness that being around people I didn't want to know invited.

Riding, I let my mind unravel until there were no images of drug growers or strange men picking up hitchhikers. It unraveled, like a spool that has fallen from the sewing machine, into nothing but a clumped mess. I rid myself of the aneurism-inducing worries and concerns over what had ever been said or done to me. I threw the tangential, meandering thoughts away that were not drawn through the hooks and needle but wadded up and choked the machine.

The little girl I had been wanted me to protect her, and I hadn't done a very good job of that these last few years. I hadn't protected that innocent girl when I was younger, I realized.

"Woh!" I was yelling before I was thinking. We had been cantering along, unperturbed, until I had missed the rhythm of the ride and pushed down with my rump when I should have been bouncing up. Trying to counteract my downward thrust, White Stripe had bucked. Immediately afterwards, he had found he couldn't propel us forward in the same way and had halted his advance.

"Woh," I said again, soothingly. He was trotting like a Tennessee walker horse, gnawing at the bit. I pulled the reins lightly, requesting he come to a complete standstill. Before he had ceased movement completely, I had slipped a leg over the saddle and taken my feet from the stirrups. I slid down from the saddle with as little pressure on him as possible while putting the saddlebags back on him.

I walked with him a moment until he was looking at me, still biting the metal bit. I gazed at him and yawned, letting him know there was no danger. He nodded his head, pulling on the reins and adjusting his bridle as he did so. I had been about to hold the reins, but instead, I went to the saddlebag and pulled out his halter and lead rope.

"Let's do this," I said as I unbuckled a few straps on the bridle. He raised his head unexpectedly, but I knew it was a matter of finding comfort, not worry or concern, as I slipped the bridle off of his head and moved the reins from his shoulders, past his neck and then down, past his face. I placed it all on a jutting piece of leather from the saddlebag near me. He ducked into the halter and I pushed the single buckle together. He bumped my shoulder with his cheek as I held the lead rope and looked forwards, to where we were walking. I noticed a sign on the trail that had a black picture of a horse with a red circle around it, next to similar pictures of bicyclists and walkers with poles. We were in the right area, which had concerned me as we set out earlier, because many trails were not horse friendly, we were lucky to have found ones that were.

The sun was hot from its position directly above us, casting few shadows and torturing us both. "Only mad dogs and Englishmen go out in the noonday sun." I looked at White Stripe as I spoke, "That's an Indian proverb."

He shook his head and pulled my arm holding the lead rope as he did. The heat felt like it was making noises and I wiped my brow, tasting sweat trickle into the corners of my mouth as I did.

"Do you want to know what gets me through the day?" I asked White Stripe. "Being a horse, of course you want to know, you just love to have conversations!" He did not respond, but I saw the damp, dark marks of sweat spread out from under the saddle and bags on him. Worried, I continued speaking, "Quotes and proverbs." I said, "Quotes and proverbs! Here's one: 'It is by riding a bicycle that you learn the contours of a country best, since you have to sweat up the hills and coast down them.'"

I looked around us, at this very flat valley we had been riding in for a while, "Hemingway didn't say anything about sweating up the flat bits. It's still quite awful. I really do love this side of California, but the more miles you get away from the ocean, the more awful the terrain seems to get. Come on, let's go find some campground or something near the ocean."

I said to him as I led him through a narrow part of a downed fence, "Understand that getting distracted by emotional or cognitive irrelevancies leads to rational failure, Pony, where you can't understand logic. That's what I did, back there," I told him as he snorted out mucus on my shoulder, "and it looks like you agree."

I giggled as I tapped my fingers on the light stripe of his nose, "Good pony to wait," I cooed, like an overprotective mother at the highway.

I hooked my foot into the stirrup and held the center of the saddle, pulling myself up as quickly as I could to avoid hurting him for too long as I used his body. His bridles was still hanging from the saddlebag. I felt like there was something I had been thinking about, something I had done before getting off the saddle last, that I needed to re-examine, but it felt like a smell of a dinner that had already been eaten, an ephemeral thought that would only come back to me when I wasn't ready or looking for it.

"What's this?" I said, seeing a red metal road block to our right. "That's a fire trail!" I said, knowing now how fire trails led to rivers. "Let's go!" I said, guiding him around the gate and spurring him into action downward. We followed the dirt road, full of bumps and turns, and reached a trail that paralleled a fortified creek. Plants and trees abounded around us, now, and I took the saddle off of him and let him guzzle the water from his place on a sand bank. I tucked my feet out of my shoes and jumped down from the big rocks that lined the road to the smaller ones that lined the creek and squatted at the water's edge. I cupped my hands at it and let it fall into my mouth and run down my chin. I felt it pass tiny hairs below my mouth and I purposefully felt the stubble I was growing on my face.

"I'm becoming a man!" I said, looking at White Stripe, but looked down, away from him, speaking to myself, now, "Why am I becoming a man?" My face had cooled, but I felt hot lines of tears spring from my eyes and create burning trails down my cheeks. They married with the water from the creek still on my chin and jumped from my face, into the creek. I wasn't necessarily upset, I thought, which made me cry harder, because I was more disconcerted than angry. I put my hands under my eyes and shook my head, because that confusion led to a brooding anxiousness that did make me upset. I was worried. I was very worried for myself.

I heard a splash and gradually raised my head. Without hurrying, I looked to see White Stripe testing the water with his hoof. He was pawing at the sand, then stepping forward without reluctance. He looked around the stream, then his face jutted forward when his eyes had settled on me. He looked down at his hooves and began discerning the safest path towards me.

When he was a yard away from me, he elongated his neck and opened his mouth, nipping at the air in front of my face with his tongue sprawled over his bottom teeth. He put his velvety lips around my shoulder and raked his I extended a hand towards his face and he retracted his entire head quickly, then snorted and pushed it back to me. He pushed his nose into my palm.

I began to get up and he tilted his neck, perhaps trying to pull my hand with him. I held onto one side of his halter and lifted my body up from its crouched position with the other. He swung his neck, controlling me as I used his force to jump. I landed with only one foot as he pushed his eye into my shoulder. I rubbed his chin, following the crescent curve with my fingers and patted his neck with the other hand.

A rock skittered down the stream and I saw him jump away from me, every leg in the air, like I had seen Lippizaners do. I laughed and the shock of seeing him do something so extraordinary made me fall on my own backside. He trotted towards me in the water, halting just in front of me, and rubbed his soaked, grimy nose against my face.

Trying to avert getting any more of his snout's snot, I ducked my face into my shoulder, "No more, that's gross!" I wiped it on my shirt, saying, "Gross, gross, gross."

I wiped my face on my shirt. Realizing all of my clothes were soaked, I stripped them off and bundled them up on one of the rocks. I splashed water onto White Stripe, making sure to rub a hand down his legs, checking for any scrapes or blood. I pushed into his belly gently with my hands, feeling the normal shifting and making sure there weren't any masses in his stomach that weren't digesting. Colic struck hard and fast, especially in horses, and I didn't want to run the risk of letting him eat all of the wild grasses and greens he wanted until he couldn't pass one of them and keeled over, dead.

At the thought of what I was avoiding by testing his health, I put an arm over his back and pressed my head to his chest. I heard all of the wonderful sounds of life passing through him. Nothing would completely allay my fears, but I was alleviated by the simple way the vital spirit was moving through him.

Abruptly, he moved out of the water and began searching out food to munch from the bank. I raced after him and surveyed the flowers and greens around us. There was always a chance there was something I did not see or know about, but the main contenders for poisonous plants were not present and so, I returned to the water.

The creek was not deep enough to swim in, but I could sit on the sandy bottom, letting my long legs drag in the water's pull. I studied them, seeing how they looked more like frog legs than human legs when I compared them to the image I had of my sturdier female legs. These ones almost looked breakable. I hadn't been jumping and sliding and using my legs the way I had as a woman, but I had a suspicion that if I did they would snap more easily. The dark hairs that sprouted on them did not seem out-of-place like hair seemed before on my previous legs, and I got the overall sense that I could let a lot of things go, like the hair on my underarms and groin, with fewer repercussions. But what were the repercussions? Before, as a female, I had felt a prowess over my body; controlling it, taming it, sculpting it, even. Now, I felt like the potential for my body would be met with or without my ever-present jurisdiction over it.

I wondered if I would begin being predatory like a lot of boys and men can be, and that thought bemused me. I had almost completely accepted that behavior from them as a woman, placing a high importance on being accepting rather than disregarding the people that exhibited that behavior. Now, as a man, I was made aware of the very blatant choice I was giving myself. I was asking myself to not be exploitive, right here and now.

What happened when I was not in a calm, comfortable setting and I was reacting quickly, I asked myself. I feared acting on impulse, being exploitative, rapacious, vulturous. I was informed, I had been a woman, and if even I could not control myself, as so many men claimed they couldn't, I would count myself just as loathsome as them. The abuse of power many men imposed on women could result in their demise, in the worst case. My radical premonitions were making me look at the sky with dejected eyes, and I breathed out, asking myself to close the door on the thoughts.

"'Be not self-willed,'" I completed a couplet from a Shakespearean sonnet by saying, "'For thou art much too fair to be death's conquest and make worms thine heir.'"

I had spoken the words so many times to myself before that I felt like it was a tactic that preserved me in a new and different way. Like magic, the words had sedated the deteriorations of my thoughts and I laid back in the water, letting the cold water pass over my face and torso.

The warmth of the day had loosened my body and now, as the frigid water passed over it, it was gripped, became tightened, and felt hypothermic. The water wasn't more than chilly and I laid out fully, sprawling and turning like a seal in the water. I didn't understand why, but I felt incapacitated in the water, unable to move up, once I pushed myself down below the surface.

I breathed in underwater, choking on a small amount of water quickly. Something told me to breathe in, even if I was underwater. I gagged out, my eyes closing as tears sprung out and dispersed in the water. In an arduous motion I took a deeper breath, gulping down the water and noticing a smile crease up to my eyes as I looked around me with wide eyes, now. Instinctually, I breathed in again, getting a new gulp of water and feeling its weight in my lungs. I had the idea to thrash my limbs, call for my horse's help, but I was debilitated and none of those things happened. Instead, on my third breath, I started to feel my muscles and body getting the oxygen they needed. Somehow, my mind told my body that it was okay to breathe. I did, gulping in the fluid through my mouth and letting it pass down.

My body ached, suddenly forcing me to think I was drowning, but I gripped the sand under my body with my hands and pulled myself deeper into the water. I gulped in more water and felt it pass down, into my lungs, which were heavier than they had ever been. I breathed in again and, though my sternum felt stressed and crushed, there was no actual pain. The water streamed around my head and back and I opened my eyes as I breathed regularly. I laughed to myself, shaking my head, and pulled myself up the stream, grabbing rocks and pushing off of the sand bottom. I remembered times as a child, swimming next to my mother in pools, nothing as hazardous as a stream in the middle of nowhere. But as I swam loops down into the pool here, I felt connected with her, like I was swimming with her, now. The frivolity of the memory was sweet in my mind and I let myself pretend she was next to me, now.

I gulped in again, smiling as I realized the water in my lungs and throat was effortlessly flowing into and out of me. I kept my mouth open as I did when I breathed when I ran or, sometimes, when I slept. It became second-nature to breathe in and out and the light from the bright sky faded as I worked to find the bottom of the pool.

Fear gripped me as I explored the seemingly limitless depths, possessing me and asking me to raise myself, remove myself, anything. I pushed past that fear, like I was pushing past the burn of my thighs or a side cramp during a run. I worried about silly things, like the bends, which I knew were from greater depths than this, but the fear still gnawed at me. I worried about monsters lurking in the depths of this river pool, which made me chuckle to myself as I kicked the water and tried to go deeper, still. I worried about White Stripe and, finally, I had something realistic to force me to raise myself up.

I rose slower than the slowest air bubble, pulling myself up until the surface was only a ceiling above me, a warped glass ceiling that was volatile and unstable and ever-shifting. I punched through it with my head, my gasp of air a distinctively masculine sound as I began choking and puking up all of the water that had been inhabiting my lungs. I felt my eyebrows push together and I could feel sobs escaping me as new tears pushed forth from my eyes. I continued puking water, two full lungs and a throat full of it, until I felt viscous mucous painting onto my tongue and over my lips. I wiped my chin of it, then pushed water from the stream onto my face, shaking my head and kicking my legs to stay afloat. I looked to my right and White Stripe was staring directly at me from the shore. His ears twitched when we made eye contact and he did not lower his head.

"Hey, pony," I said as I swam with my arms flapping in the water like a bird in flight. His white stripe moved vertically as he bobbed his head up and down. I pulled myself out of the water and, careful not to slip on rocks, approached him. I laid a hand on his head, steadying him. I walked down the stream trail with him and picked up my clothes, threw them on, then got his saddle back on him and got back on it quickly. I smoothed a palm over his neck, carrying my fingers over his ruddy brown hairs, then brought that hand to my face, gripping my lips with my fingers. I thought for moments over how scared I had been and how little I knew about what had just happened. I clicked my tongue and continued White Stripe south on the trail, cantering past dense brush and sprawling fields.

Intuitively, I crossed a bridge and saw trail markers with little hiker's feet and mileages on it. When I began to see tire tracks and fence posts, I knew we were onto something.

"Woh, boy," I said as I saw a tiny little booth next to a dirt parking lot and asphalt road on either side of it. I dismounted him and pulled him by the reins.

"Hey there," I heard someone good-naturedly say from the booth.

"Hiya!" I responded and turned the corner of the stall towards the opening.

"How are you doing today?" the woman in there asked.

"I am-"

"You look confused."

"-confused. Yes, that is what I was going to say. I can breathe," I didn't know how I should phrase it, but said it straight-forwardly, "underwater."

"Because of the perfluocarbon that runs in fresh water, yes."

I looked up, then down.

"You still look confused," she said, standing up.

"That's because I am."

She approached White Stripe and me and pointed to him with a questioning glance. I nodded up and down and she nodded, approached him, and put a hand on his mane, petting it awkwardly.

"So, what makes it breathable?"

She eyed me, then said, "Oxygen-rich water flows freely. Until it hits the ocean or becomes compromised in a standing body of water like a lake, it is completely breathable. You just have to get over the gag-reflex," she laughed and closed her eyes a bit as her face scrunched in an emotion I didn't know very well.

"Crazy," I said, looking towards the path from the river.

"You have really never heard of it?" I shook my head. "Well, it is something else, at any rate," she said, twisting a curly black hair on her index finger.

"Is this a new event?"

She shrugged her thick shoulders, curly black hair cascading around them as she spoke, "Always has been this way. Do you want a tour of the park?"

By habit, I replied, "No."

"Well, then," she sated tersely.

"Is there camping?" I asked.

"Sure is, for twenty bucks a night."

"That'll be fine." I took out the cash I had and gave it to her. She looked at it speculatively, a large wad in her hands, then counted it.

"How many nights do you plan on staying here?"

"Not too many, but I don't like carrying cash around with me. I have enough food and stuff. I just need a place to rest my head, away from it all."

"Aw, away from it all," she said. "Big city guys always like to get away from it all."

I held up my palms to her, "Honey, I have calluses in every knook and cranny. There isn't a thing about me that is big city."

She smirked as she looked at my hands and I watched something register in her eyes as they worked up my forearms, biceps, shoulders, and to my face. She nodded slightly as she looked at me and I felt sexualized like I did when I was a woman, but I remembered that I had habitually felt threatened as a woman, so I made sure to nod to her politely. I tipped my hat and bit my lip, making sure she knew I wasn't looking at her the way she was looking at me, out of politeness.

"Where are you staying on the park property?" I heard her ask.

"By the pool in the stream just north of here," I told her.

"You get on over there and, remember, park rangers can come in and check on you whenever they feel like it."

I looked at her, sizing up her spunk, "Is that right?"

"Oh yeah, any time, maybe even at night. You don't know." I looked at her, trying to read her mind, but her eyes were old, unbluffed, unreadable.

I was unable to speak above a mutter, "I don't know, do I?"

The auspicious look twinkled and was gone after she had said, "You have a good day, now."

"And the same goes to you," I said. I used a nearby wood stump to get on him quickly and pushed him back the way we had come. Something about the way I rode in the seat felt uncomfortable. We were trotting until when we had gone back over the bridge and then I let him carry me with a canter. Once we were out of sight, and I felt like I was not being watched, I dug my hand past my belt and jeans to adjust my boner, which was falling in an unlikely and uncomfortable way.

"Right here, boy," I said as I unslung my feet from the stirrups and landed. Before I was steadied, I started unbuckling the saddle and bags, moving onto the bridle and rifling in one of the bags to get his halter and lead. His saddle pad had salt from his sweat dried like a curving wave approaches the beach and was well-used. I staked him up and worked on creating a barrier to keep him in, then washed down the pieces of equipment as best I could, polishing the saddle and setting the pad out to dry.

After that, I rifled even more in the bags, taking a considerable amount of supplies out that would be useful. In the bottom of the first bag I began exploring was a tent, a double-wide sleeping pad, and other necessities for a camp. I began pushing the poles into one another with a system that proved effectual. They slid into the loops outfitted on the nylon of the tent. It was impressive, if only some fixed clothe that hung limply from plastic, but I was excited to put my belongings and clothes inside of it. I outfitted the bedding as best I could with thicker pants and jackets of mine, as well as the clothe that went under the saddle. Laying on it to test it wasn't opulent, but I wasn't too privileged to sleep on it later that night. I exited the green, translucent light from the tent and looked at the fading light.

"Fire?" I asked White Stripe. He had been dozing, but I untied his lead rope from the stake and tied it to the opposing side of his halter instead. I slung the saddlebags over his shoulders and used a rock to get up on him. Clicking my tongue, he got the idea and began to trot away from the creek, to the East. I scanned the ground for dead logs but there were only small tinder branches. We approached a meadow and I tightened my hold on his ribs with my legs.

He knew me well enough to know I wanted to canter and, without me having to kick him, he began. Riding without a saddle, I had to be both more loose and more rigid. I could not be afraid to let my butt completely rise and fall, but I also had to grip from the knees and lower and grip from there. When he seemed hesitant or hiccuped in his stride, I had to make the decision whether I would plummet back down quickly or stay risen and wait for his gate to return. It took much more thought than normal riding and I was happy to spot wood at the other edge of the meadow and slide my leg over to meet the other one. I rode side-saddle like that for half of a moment before he halted and I slid off fully. I started snapping wood over my knee immediately and he stood by me, nosing the dirt and becoming bored quickly. I loaded the one side of the empty saddle bag with wood and held his spine to get back on him. He exhaled and turned around, trotting nervously back into the meadow.

"That was good, boy," I said as I pushed my weight down lackadaisically and he walked slowly with me atop him. The long grass of the meadow swayed slowly, with a heavy languor that made me feel there was no other type of afternoon other than this one. The golden stubs reached his shoulders in some places, and dipped down to barely brush his legs in others and I could feel his yearning to eat them. I allowed him the pleasure of dipping his head down low to munch on the dry grass.

Because the saddlebags were in front of me, rather than behind, there was space behind me and I laid back on him. I was at once facing the odd, nearly green sky. Its clouds formed layers, cascading away in grays and whites that I could never paint nor reproduce. My hand was in front of my vision, tracing the outlines of them as they shifted and swayed with the wind currents. From my throat sprouted a song, one I had never heard filled with tremors and hesitations as I sought the words that rhymed and completed my thoughts. When I was done, I felt open and empty of the hinderances and ideas that had been occupying my thoughts without helping much of anything inside me. I sang again, driving out the same words with a different melody. I felt White Stripe shift and sat up to see him turned around, looking to me. I smiled, feeling the wind tunnel into between my tonsils and cheeks as I did. I closed my eyes and nodded and White Stripe walked on, towards the camp. I set the dry wood up in a hole I had dug out in a bed and lit the dry grass on fire with a match from the saddlebag. As I searched out matches, I found a cooking pot, a bag of rice, and most surprising of all, a packet of applewood sausage. I shook my head out, amazed.

I cooked dinner and slept restlessly, letting the flapping tent and howling wind push me from sleep. I thought shallowly, never able to push past the surface of thought. I felt like a cat, going into the forest and escaping humanity, whereas the wolf knew to go into humanity, to feel its pains and pleasures and evolve with them. I felt a deep yearning in me to rectify something I was ruining, without knowing what it was that I had been letting fall into disrepair.

The morning gave me no equanimity that I knew how to hold onto and I busied myself. I patted White Stripe and staked a tether in the meadow, letting him graze there as I gathered fire wood for the day and set about building a better encampment. For the time being, I told myself, I would live down by the river. The stigmas I felt surrounding it dissolved as I thought about the good I had seen people around me establish. My dad and teachers were the best examples I had of why I should disregard the life of convention. Their position in society of a habitually employed and forever fixed member of the workforce held a place of contempt in my mind. Contracted to larger schemas that I knew a trifling bit about, we seemed to remain in a state of fatigue and inundation when committed to other peoples' dreams. And never able to attain our own, as well. Wanting not that for myself, I resigned myself to living like this.

The morning stew of barley from the saddlebags and dandelion roots I had found left a good deal to the imagination in order to be consumed, but I guzzled it regardless. I tied up the food Robert had given me and hoisted it on a lead rope to a tree branch and pushed an extra layer onto my torso and I set out on a walk after re-checking White Stipe's stake.

I passed over rocks and jumped a chasm across the creek to explore the forest to the west of it. Light glittered from the tree coverage above and I heard the songs of birds. I felt like I had been moving too fast when riding White Stripe to hear these sounds, or perhaps he scared them too much for them to chirp and sing around him. Muscles long-since unused felt restored and stimulated as I pushed past greens and rocks. My thighs itched where blood was finding new routes in the veins and arteries. My hands slapped them and I continued without allowing myself second or third thoughts.

Early dawn let in splaying panels of light, breeching the dusky olive of the morning sky and paralyzing in it the soft cold that chilled only the joints of my fingers and toes. I stretched them to look up and see a black silhouette before me. With an angle of the neck, the stag pushed with its shoulders to lift its mighty head against the milky jade of first light.

After a twitch of the nose, he exhaled and his silhouette alighted in front of his vibrant breathe. The iridescent spectrum that splayed from his breathe carried into the daybreak's colorless ambient fog and then was saturated in white light. He breathed out again and the steam from his belly and throat was fleetingly colorful before it blanched and vanished. The sight was satisfying, with a piquancy about it that I wanted to hold onto, but its ephemeral nature moved off my tongue and my palette seemed to changed almost immediately after it had vanished from it.

"You again," came a voice of a woman and I stopped searching the forest. "You happy to see me or is that just fear?"

My eyes settled on the park ranger I had met the previous day.

I looked at her, smiling weakly, "Happy to see you."

"Likewise," she said as she walked towards me from a trail I had been near. As she did, I noticed the way her dusty green pants bunched up at the top. I was breathing out of my mouth, jaw slack, and I felt myself pressuring it to close. I looked up, at her eyes, flustered. I saw some special cognizance in her eyes as she cocked her head at me, smiling.

"I didn't get your name yesterday, did I?"

"Iliza." she said.

"Iliza, nice," was all I could muster.

"And you are?"

"Uh," I raised my hand to scratch the back of my neck, "Ashna."

"Promise not to tell?" she asked me.

I splayed out my hands, sucking in my spit, and said, "Tell what?" I felt a disquietude spread around us and birds stopped hitting sticks together and bellowing out their songs. She approached me further until I noticed the long slope of her nose and the way her black curls bunched until they fell over her shoulders. I followed the trail of her hair and let my eyes fall on the way her chest was pressing out of her uniform. Without willing it, I was thinking of how much her body was being contained by the green apparel. Her shiny badge blocked my view of a tiny swathe of fabric, but I knew it was bulging there, too.

She was bringing her face close to mine and I felt the hot breathe of air on my face as she spoke the words, "Tell anybody about this." She had a hand around my back and with the other, was unfastening my belt. I was breathing hard, worried I would betray indifference or interrupt her in any way. She had pulled my pants down and, feeling me with a hand, she looked at me, opening her mouth and gasping. My eyebrows raised and I tried to smile.

"You don't mind, do you?"

"Me?" I asked, "No, of course, not. Go ahead." I was almost muttering and I clenched my jaw to stop myself from talking too much. I held one of her hands as she bent at the knees and her voice muffled as her hot mouth encircled me. I gasped and I could feel her smile, then she lifted both hands in a circle in front of her mouth.

I looked down to see her chest rising and falling as she tilted her head. I couldn't help the gasp that ensued. I almost shook, my back angled and I breathed in unexpectedly.

"I want you to feel," she said as she put her hand on my thigh, moving it up, "my wet," I saw a smile play across her mouth before she continued, "tongue," her fingers made circles against my jeans, "down here,"

"You don't have to-" I began to say.

"What?" she looked at me, hurt forming rings around her eyes.

"I just don't want to be advantageous or take advantage of your-"

"You're ruining the mood," she said, unbuttoning her top button. Her green collar sagged. The second and third and fourth buttons were all a blur as they were unbuttoned because my hands were around her.

"I don't just want to see your breasts," I muttered, "I want to see your best, too."

"But you want to see them, too, right?"

"Oh, oh yes," I said as I realized she was unclasping her bra. I slipped my hands under one side and alternated squeezing and releasing the mass in my hands. I shuddered as I bent to hold it in my mouth and feel the soft texture with my tongue. Meeting the warmth of her flesh with my tongue, I held it longingly and slipped off my pants fully.

"I want you inside me, now," she whispered down to me. I nodded, removing myself from her nipple and beginning to unclasp her tight belt. Her button was ready to pop out and I glided the zipper down quickly. She kicked off her shoes and I counted to ten to halt my impatience as I pulled her pants down fully, taking them around both of her feet.

She leaned against a fallen log and I glided my hand over her pale, solid thighs. One hand held her at the lower back and I cradled her body in my hands as I gently moved my other hand closer to her inner thigh, moving up, then nervously back down. Her breathing accelerated, then halted, only to rebound again. I shook my head and bent down to nudge her with my nose, then pull her underwear aside to lick her gently. Her hand grabbed my hair as I nodded my head into her, pushing deeper in with my tongue. My hand gently moved under my chin and my index, then middle fingers found places to touch alongside my tongue.

"Down," she said, pointing to a bare area on the ground.

I laid back and she put a leg to either side of my hips. One of her hands held her hip and the other was finding a path down her navel. She pushed them down until she was touching me, tugging on my shirt.

My hands flailed as I tried to cover my chest up with my hands as I was whimpering, "No, no, no." I watched her flex her legs, grinding against my leg with the cotton of her panties just skimming my thigh, then pushing up on my hip.

"What's wrong?" she asked.

I bit my lip and shook my head, smiling at her. She nodded as she dipped down, touching her chest to mine. Her hips dipped down to press against mine, the bones softly grinding against one another. She lifted her butt into the air and the cool air from the forest grazed against the inner part of my thighs that had been moistened by her. It made me shiver and she dipped her pelvis down again and the moisture touched me in a way I could feel. Her hand, that had been on my shoulder, moved down my chest, pushing between our bodies until she was touching me and pushing me into her.

Suddenly, and unexpectedly I was immersed.

I looked from her to the forest above us. Light splashed from the openings between leaves and as the wind swayed the branches, it moved from my face, then away. The dapple lighting played against Iliza's skin, making intoxicatingly beautiful patterns that were almsot at-once, gone. I felt a need to keep watching to the simplicity. My eyes were ajar for the display, teeth clenched like I couldn't risk resting my features for fear that that would cause some demise.

Without warning or expectation, I was suspended. While Iliza pushed and pulled her body on me, like water crashing in and receding on a sandy beach, I became detached, existing in some very far place with only the impression of light. Subtle white light, carrying with it the sensation of warmth, affection, ardor, desire, and the sensation of tenderness.

My eyes were closed, then, and a great rocking and shaking from my spine broke me from my reverie. I had never cum as a man before, and it was momentarily very worrisome for it was a very different feeling from what I was used to. Instead of being wrapped up in ideas and thoughts, my body was distinct from the soul, mind, or psyche. I was soma, I was only my anatomy, nothing more. I was the shaking of my jaw, to the bunching of my ribs, to the convulsion of my butt, to the spasmodic shaking I was feeling in my groin, until it was out of me, uncontrollably forced into Iliza as her hand moved from her breast to touch my stomach.

I glimpsed her eyes widen and, too tired to smile, the edges on the outside of her eyes creased into happy crow's feet. Her hair hung limply in sweaty tendrils and beads of sweat had formed beneath her neck and above her lips. I breathed in, hoping to begin words or remarks, but realized there was nothing in me that could. Because it was convenient, I lifted a hand and patted her hip, commending what she had done.

She tilted her head and smiled and I moved my hand to my face, sighing exhaustedly into my palm.

"Thank you, really, I've never had it like that," I told her.

I heard her giggle and say, "Well isn't that something. How old are you?"

I exhaled, saying, "Twenty-two."

"I'll be," she said, elongating her words as she held by age in esteem.

"And you?"

"Five years your senior."

I opened my eyes when she said, removing my hand from over them, to tell her, "I thought you were much younger, you look my age."

"Let me see your camp," she said, pushing up from my body as she eyed me.

"To see if it is up to code?"

"To know where I'm going tonight."

"Righty-o, Miss."

"I know it's a little late for this, Ashna, but I was wondering if you've been-"

I read her mind and spoke quickly, "After every partner, yeah."

"Wow, that's a relief. My standard practice is along very similar lines."

"Meaning?"

"You're safe."

"Good conversation to have," I said, "Good to know it's not any different in this world."

"What world is that, exactly?"

I stuttered, "The national park world, of course!"

She blinked, then raised her eyebrows, "Lead the way."

My heart had begun to feel anxious at the suspicion that something had happened to White Stripe. I was anxious that something unrelated had gone wrong with him after I had been committing a dirty act, and so I had to calm my nerves and tell myself it was stress for naught. Nevertheless, I breathed easier when I saw him.

"Nice job here," she said, "but if it rains you're screwed."

"I can hang out with you, then."

She laughed and said, "It'll be like we're taking one big shower."

"Hey, yeah."

"So we're not about to become soul mates, right?"

"I'm a bit against this idea that there's only one person you're meant to be with and they complete you."

"Yeah, me, too," she agreed.

"But at the same time, we can't claim to know or not know everything. Maybe you're drawn to certain people because both of your atoms were near one another during the creation of the universe or some star exploding and those atoms keep being drawn back together."

"That's a theory?"

"Working theory." I smiled, "I get what you're saying, but I think it makes me a bit worried thinking that we're just hooking up. It seems irresponsible."

"Well, there is some attraction here, but I'm not attracted to long-term relationships. Especially with vagrants," she said, looking me up and down in faux-disapproval.

"You don't really mean that?" I laughed, but felt cut up inside.

"No, of course not. You're one hell of a man." She touched my cheek and I remembered that it was wholly impossible for someone to accept me for who I was while I was a man. I ducked my head, hiding the sadness in my eyes from her.

"Do you mind if I come by tonight?"

"Please do." I said, "Should I make some extra gruel for you?"

"No need, I have my own snack reserved. See you," she said.

"Bye."

CHAPTER EIGHT

She stayed true to her word and visited me, making the monotony of that night and many more in the following weeks less present. There was a repetition to setting up my fires and meals and watching the earth move that was broken up by her visits.

"You have some skills at this," she told me as we sat around my campfire on fallen logs that I had pulled from the forest floor.

"Thanks, I like something about it," I told her.

She asked, "You're not a true wilderness man, are you?"

I laughed it off, "Neither of those things."

She sighed, "If only…."

"Hey, I know what that sighing is all about."

She looked up, "What, you think I have someone else I'm thinking of?"

I smiled widely, my words coming out from between my teeth as I held the smile up to her, "Well if there was any doubt before-"

She held her arms up high, "I don't know what to think, really. I like him, he knows it, but nothing's happened. Being friends is something else, entirely."

"If in friends you do not find truth, or the truth hurts you, the future does not hold your friendship," I scratched my arm as I talked and became more relatable by saying, "I've been inside the head of a man for awhile now, but I can't say too much that'll help."

"You've been a huge help, actually," she said, "by treating me like the woman I deserve to be treated like."

I blushed and pushed forward, "So you say he is a wilderness man?"

"He works in the park."

"What was his excuse? You're a beautiful woman, and sometimes there is a very good reason."

"Sometimes there's not. He said he really liked me and that I was right that he wanted to date me, but, then he stopped talking to me for days," she looked at me directly, her eyes wirling pools, before looking down and away.

"Ask him again, but let him know that anything he has going on that would get in the way of you two doesn't matter."

"I'll try, I will."

"But, now that I know you're interested in someone else, it feels almost wrong to have sex with you."

"Quite frank, aren't you?"

"I am. I like to have sex with people that really want to have sex with me, and even if I really want to have sex with you, that's not enough. I need to know your heart and head's in it."

"You can afford to be picky?"

"I'm just not willing to make mistakes that will hurt later, I guess."

She smiled and said, "Well, I guess I could lie to you and tell you I have eyes for only you, but for being such a gentleman and all, I'll treat you with the same respect you've treated me. Mind if I come back and talk?"

"Aw," I said jokingly, "You like me, you really do, just in a different way."

She grew serious, "There's something about you I really relate to and it means a lot to me to have a friendship with you." I smiled and held her hand, forcing myself to forget about the way I could have taken advantage of her by having been a woman. I consciously decided to just enjoy the tie I had with her and poked at the fire with a stick from the ground.

"You know," I said, "I used to be afraid that I was so apathetic that it hurt other people."

"You're not apathetic, at all."

"Really?"

"No, you really care, quite a bit. Maybe too much. Maybe that's your weakness."

I furrowed my brow. I had been happy to have a conversation centered around my attributes, but it had quickly turned. "What do you mean?"

"You could have really made me think only of you and devote myself." I squinted at the word choice- I would have no devotional friendships, if I could help it. "But, you cared about me and talked to me about what I really cared about, which wasn't yet me. Do you know what I mean?"

"I guess I do. Want to get some more wood?"

She nodded, "Sounds good."

In the mornings, when the long grass was shiny from dew, White Stripe and I would be disturbed by the steady parade of deer, marching their slow and wary way. I watched them come and leave the meadow over my cup of cowboy coffee I had made by boiling water and coffee grounds and strolled to where they had sauntered. Where they had walked, the dew had been pressed or wiped away and there were tiny dulling trails.

I found myself following the paths. In the forest I could tell the deer had been there because the ground coverage was all but gone in a narrow path. I followed deer trails for the first time, finding I broke and snapped branches they merely passed. I found the places where they had broken brush and walked so far along their trail that I began to recognize the trails they used often and ones that had only been used once, where the brush was broken down instead of made sparse by continual use.

I climbed the redwoods, finding myself one morning forty feet in the air, and the next, in a sudden burst of confidence, nearly a hundred. I sat there for a long time, looking over the wind rustling and moving up and down entire swathes of trees. Their shadows and highlights became images I wanted to watch for lifetimes. As I stayed up there, I began to think I was able to see even the slow progression of the earth move. I had studied the wind's movements, and I knew it was not just that that I was observing. I was also seeing the slow progression of the planet as I moved atop one of its trees. It shifted, and so did the tree, and so did I. I felt appreciative, not knowing if I was humbled or felt added composure because of what I was able to witness.

I talked to Iliza one last time, starting by saying, "You know, when you feel everything for a person, you are giving yourself reason to feel nothing for anyone in the future."

"You're not talking about how much I like you, are you?" she asked.

"No, your crush."

Her voice was heavy, "Oh, that."

"How is it going?"

"I think knowing you as a friend was very helpful. Opening up to others is made less difficult when they open up to you, though."

"It is," I said. "I'm glad you wanted to with me."

"I just wish he would with me," she said.

"If I leave, you might just find a way to fill the hole in your heart I was filling with him," I said.

"I don't wan to go jumping from man to man," she looked at me, then tilted her chin down onto her shoulder and looked away, at the shifting forest. I looked at the part of the forest her eyes were trained to. Leaves fanned out onto one another, their oblong shapes intersecting for brief moments before the wind pulled them apart, only to be pushed back together and for their palettes to coalesce, again.

"Right now, you know what you want. That happens to be a man. That doesn't mean a thing about you. That doesn't give anyone the right to put a derogatory label on you, including yourself."

The push and pull of the leaves of the forest reminded me of an ocean tide sweeping across the sand of a beach. Pulling apart and joining with it, cyclically and forever, to no ends. Only the things created by the two merging were free. The bubble and foam from the ocean against the beach evaporated. The sound of leaves scraping and massaging against one another wafted from the branches and to our ears.

We hugged goodbye and I felt the happy pull on my heart.

"You'll still be here in the future?" I asked her.

"Always will be," Iliza said.

"I'll see you again."

"I hope you do, you're a very good man."

I laughed and grabbed the reins. I was surprised by the connection you can have with complete strangers. There was a way we both looked at each other, happy to know one another existed even if we never saw one another, ever again.

Chapter nine

The hair of his mane both flowed outward and snapped inward on itself as we rode. One moment it looked like thousand of tentacles writhing, then as his head pushed down and his back legs hurtled forward, it was a thick sheet, slightly tussled from the night before. With my left hand clenched around nothing but its own flesh, I took a second to lift it from the nook of my waist and lifted the fingers to open and close on his hair cautiously. I kept my eyes on the ground and his body, but concentrated on loosening the reins as much as I could and holding onto a large tuft of hair with my left. He shook out his neck, whinnying shrilly, and, for a second, I thought I would soon be hurtling in the air as he fell, but he was simply braking and slowing to a canter.

"Ay," I said as I registered his change of motion, pushing my heels, which were already tight against his flank, deeper into his side. He tossed his head and pushed back into the red dirt to gallop again.

The straightaway of dirt and small brush seemed to narrow and would eventually end. I slowed him when I realized we would have to be turning west soon and for a quarter of a mile, kept him in a mellow trot. Because the gallop had made him so limber, his gait was smooth and not as jostling as it had been earlier in the day, when we had left.

We were high up, able to look down from our position onto a large swathe of land, flowing out around us, not at all dissimilar to the inexhaustible yearning I had to keep going, to keep moving.

Thinking of what was below the ensuing mountain pass, I watched for a trail leading out and down onto a vast valley overlook. We continued to curve and twist with the road as it found a way to bring us into a slow descent. I saw in the central part of the valley a small, smoldering, and aflame mass of a town. My breathe caught, but I could not look away, for there was more to see.

Through a smaller mountain pass I could dimly see a second small town, in complete conflagration. My sight of it was feeble, but it took little time to register the flames and light coming from it. Both small city's flames bushed outwards and the shimmery before the black fog above them spoke of the great fire there.

I stood back, aghast. I could not fathom completing a journey for pleasure nor pressure, now. Dead and destroyed down there were two towns: lives and DNA and people of importance were now gone. I caught myself nearly weeping in anguish when in my peripheral I could see a group- a family turned away from the destruction. I solemnly walked him to the family. They all looked up at me, then back down slowly. Only the tallest matriarch spoke, "Yes, hello."

"What is happening here?" I asked.

She said in a cracked, broken voice, "God sent down angels to find ten worthy people in these towns, but when they only found our family worthy, God sent down smite."

I hesitated to ask the matriarch, but ended up doing so, "What is the problem here. I mean to say, what were they doing?"

I was looked at mournfully, "Not having any sex."

I looked at the family, aghast again. My memory spoke faintly of the towns of Sodom and Gomorrah. Cities that had been adulterous, save but one family that had not partaken in the scandalous acts.

I hesitated, but asked, "If you had been saved while so many were persecuted, I have to ask, what were you doing if the rest of the city's families were not having sex?"

White Stripe reared and I could see them no more as his head and mane took up my frame of vision. I whistled and pulled in the reins to one side to have him turn as he landed. We were in mutual establishment to get away from them. Their mournful faces seemed to be in my mind even as I looked away. We pushed away, running together like scared children until I was too tired to keep my body moving with his and I got off. I began to walk with him, but he bent his neck and I could not move him.

"Off we go," I enthused, but he snorted at the ground. A boy doll was laying there. A soft, cloth, and very dirty one- likely from the recent devastation. His blue pants were made from jeans and his red shirt from corduroy.

"Where did they think they were going to get more children from if they didn't have sex?" I asked myself as I pocketed the doll and fed some oats to him from a saddle-bag before strapping the stirrup and getting up. We walked a few paces before a young man revealed himself from behind a tree as he swiveled on one foot, letting the other drag near the ground until it was planted in the dirt. His arms raised and he cocked his head. He held two water guns in each hand.

"Off the horse and on the ground, brother."

I was shocked, pressing my heels down slowly, hoping to push against White Stripe's withers and have us run away.

He pointed one gun down and squirted the ground. Like paper being burned, a blackness tore at the edges and smoke rose from the area. "I'm not joking around, pal."

I began to stutter as White Stripe reared, "Holy-" I raised one leg and pushed against White Stripe's flank when his front hooves had met earth, again. He began shooting his hooves against the surface of the ground as I swept us to the side of the road.

I looked back to see him finding a path parallel to ours. The sight of a man so set on violence shook fear into my spine and I held the reins steadily as I as turned, grabbing at the saddlebag. I hastily pulled on the first thing I found in the saddlebag. I kept myself level in the seat and pulled on the reins as I aimed for the man. I had to swing my arm around several times before I shot my arm towards him and let go with my hand. He gave a few startling grunts as his feet slid past his body and he fell. I slowed White Stripe completely and approached him. His hands were bound next to his thighs and he was looking around exuberantly trying to move about as he did. I pulled and he stopped.

"A lasso?!" he shouted.

I slid from the saddle and approached him, "I was just as surprised as you." I took the gun from his hands and threw it a distance away. "Anything else on you?" I asked. His face remained masked and I looked under the ankles of his pants and found one strapped in. I unhitched it from its mooring and threw it, too. I pulled the lasso and tied him around the base of a tree, then leaned back on White Stripe, watching him.

"Who are you to stick people up on some backroad?"

He grumbled angrily and I spit on the ground.

"Who are you doing this for?"

He said nothing, then looked at me, concern etching his eyes, "Will you let me go if I tell you?"

"Probably."

His head dropped before he looked up to look into my eyes with his swirling green of his, "The woman that I love."

"You'll have to do better than that," I told him, though I already felt my heart tugging on my mind to help him.

He shook his head and looked back down before saying, "It's complicated."

"You tell me all of it, now," I said, tapping my boot against the dirt and pushing my hands into my pockets.

"The first night I met her was no different from the last time I was with her when she was healthy, in that she led me the entire time. We didn't fall in love when her uncle let us use his sailboat and roam the bay or when she took me on a picnic on a mountain I had always overlooked. No, we fell in love on that first night when she grabbed my hand and took me to the backyard. When she let go and let her head rest on my chest, that's when I stopped being in love and settled into a familiar love with her. Perhaps she felt the same, but her emotions were as hard to catch as her tangled hair falling from the sky when she was on the swing set later that night, knuckles white against the chains and legs whipping athletically back and forth. Knowing what she was feeling wasn't as important as seeing how she expressed it. Do you know what I mean?"

I nodded and he continued, "Seeing her scream ecstatically before she jumped from the swing and looking down to see her soft eyes studying my face were like reading only one passage from only one book of a very long saga."

His chin leaned against the rope of the lasso as his lips quivered like feathers of a bird fluttering in an air draft. "When we began having sex, I saw the soft scar on her chest like a new thing; it was a twisted cloud hiding rain, a pendant holding some unknown ancestor's lock of hair: it was intangible to me. When she really experienced sex, she would arch her back and her scar would turn purple and the only words I thought were, 'open heart surgery' until the repetition stopped me from being able to thrust into her anymore," tears fell from his face as he swayed like a punching bag after an especially assertive roundhouse. I breathed in deeply and stopped leaning against White Stripe to squat next to him.

"When we sailed together she moved the parts beautifully with the ease of a woman born at sea. When we walked the streets she knew every route to every destination we could dream up. She pointed to trees and laughed at the squirrels and found fruit on the branches that I have never tasted before, but enjoyed feverishly as I watched the juices running down her chin, sometimes falling on her chest. Sometimes catching on her scar, like water catching on a fallen branch in a stream," he sniffed and I could see him retracing his words as he looked at me and saw the lines they had created against my face.

"I'll get to the point," he said.

"No, you're telling me so much," I said, realizing if there was a point, it was an ultimately sad one.

"That scar was a message. It was braille on her skin. It was there to tell me she was broken and that I should be gentle." He looked at me, eyes wet and mouth open and said, "I tried to be, I tried so hard to be strong and gentle. I just couldn't do both." He sucked his bottom lip into his mouth and the corners of his mouth stretched towards his ears. He breathed erratically though his nose and he opened his mouth to breathe, finally, and spoke quickly, "She had another attack and she's not doing so well, now."

I was silent, watching him, wondering what that meant in this world of opposites.

"I just want to see myself in the way she saw me, you know?"

I nodded, looking away and thinking about my mother, swimming next to me, "I know. I do. I guess, I want to know why you're out here robbing people."

He raised up his hands, "What else are you going to do?"

I reacted quickly, "Let other people live freely!"

"That's not going to happen."

I looked at him, then at the forest around us. "Where do we go?"

He looked up, disgruntled. "What do you mean?"

"I'm not just going to let you go on robbing people for money. You are trying to get money for her, right?"

He breathed in deeply and nodded, tears falling from his face, "Yes."

"Let's hitch you up. White Stripe, it looks like we have a new friend."

I stood up and grabbed my thigh as I did so, groaning at the hinderance. I began rifling through the forest, working to find his two guns. I found myself growing more and more distressed as I found myself leaving his presence. My breath caught in my throat when I thought I had found one, but hadn't. My feet slipped and I tried to noiselessly fall, but a small utterance of worry loosed itself from my lips. I could hear him moving some twenty feet away and was relieved to see the neon colored gun close by. I grabbed it and raced back to him. He was shuffling off the coil of the lasso, but stopped when he saw me holding his gun. I walked to White Stripe and grabbed some rope from the saddlebag.

"Tell me about these guns," I said as I tied his hands together.

He looked at me from the corner of his eye, then said, "Vurn 367, that's what you have in your hand. Single-release rapid fire."

"Why did you only shoot once, then?" I asked.

He looked to White Stripe, "Didn't want to hurt your horse."

"That's kind of you," I said, finishing the knot. "Do you want to tell me what's inside of it?"

"Why should I?"

"It's water, isn't it?"

"Yeah, why?"

"Your world is getting to me, that's all."

"My world?" he said, then spat on my shoe. I lifted my boot up, grimacing at it, then leaned over him.

"I've had just about enough of things I don't understand."

"I'm not hurting people because I want to, but money needs to come from somewhere."

I looked at him, speculating what to do.

"You're coming with me," I told him. I unwound the knots around the tree and held White Stripe to let him. "Get up."

"What?"

"Get on the horse," I told him. I gestured to the saddle with my head and gripped the reins tighter.

"I'm not doing that."

"I know where you can get money," I rolled my eyes, "in a way a little less illegal than this. Not much, but at least you're not overtly hurting people."

He looked up at me and his eyelids fluttered as he thought, then he nodded and smacked his lips together, "Alright, I'll do it."

"Good, I didn't want to have to impose my will on you." The thought caught in my mind and I said, again, "Impose."

We moved slowly, walking parallel to the same land I had just pushed past at a slow amble. We talked feverishly and incessantly, united in some unknown way. I sometimes looked at him with yearning in my eyes, though he was unaware of it. His glittering eyes and sharp jawline made his rogue, outlandish character all the more attractive to me, but I made no advance and in the lulls of our talking, I reminded myself of my plan to abandon him as soon as I had put him where he needed to be.

He found me a veritable wealth on knowledge when it came to the inner workings of girls and their minds and hearts.

"Why does she say it's nothing, man? Nothing's wrong one minute then the next hour we're talking and fighting about whatever it really was and it's so hard to tell what really went wrong right away."

I sighed, "That's a defense mechanism because I- they- haven't fully processed their feelings and can't accurately nor logically express their thoughts, at least not yet. So they're not going to talk about it right away because they seriously don't want to hurt you or misconstrue something. Let her tell you when she's ready, don't pressure her."

I held White Stripe's reins as we walked together. He would occasionally ask if he could get down or at least have his hands unbound, but I simply laughed, remembering the water gun I had put into the saddlebag, hoping to not need its protection. We walked on, past a church with a neon crucifix.

I laughed at the sight, the blue fluorescence of the church's name against the glowing pink outline of the cross seemed to me wrong, unnatural.

He looked at it and said, "What?"

"It's confusing to me, like choking someone while you have sex. The neon sign and the choking are supposed to heighten your excitement about religion or sex, respectively, but really they should both be enjoyable on their own. You don't need neon and you don't need fake endorphins to fall in love with the beauty of what those two things are. They are beautiful on their own. I can see a crucifix and fell no less than eighty emotions and I could feel you pushing into me and feel no less than eighty things, but when you put a façade on either, it lessens what I feel. I feel pain during sex when there should only be love and pleasure, and I feel pleasure from seeing a lighted crucifix when there should only be pain."

"What do you even mean by that?" He asked, as if my words had previously been an attempt to represent my feelings for him instead of my own, independent thoughts, about religion and desire.

"While looking at Jesus, gilded in gold and limelight, hanging from the cross, I felt only pain."

"Huh, are you-"

I shook my head, "No, not religious, but I see the worth in understanding it. And I'm sure the prophets of past were real, but I'm not going to devote myself to something I can't ever fully understand."

"Well, can you ever fully understand, say, quantum mechanics?" he asked.

"Well," I thought, "really, you can't by the time you've figured everything that exists out, there will be more created to understand."

"Exactly," he said, "consider that one hole poked in your argument."

I laughed long and loud, happy to have been proven wrong, until I asked, "What's your life story, then?"

"You don't want to hear it," I said to the ground.

"What else am I going to do up here but listen to you?"

"Fine, I don't want to tell it."

"Come on, don't be that way."

I looked up at him and blinked, "You better give me yours, first."

"I already told you about my girl," he said.

"But that's not your entire life story," I said. "I want to hear yours." I looked at him, his face shifting from one desire to the next as he thought.

"You want to hear mine?" he asked, finally, looking down with a pleased smile.

"I don't even know if you could tell it, what with all of this time we have on our hands," I said with a smile pushing past my set face.

"You really want me to tell it?" he asked, again.

"No, just tell me about someone that had an influence on you."

"Alright, I can tell that," he said.

"Take all the time you need," I said as he began talking.

"I would never admit this, but summertime is my favorite time. I remember the summer he saved me from myself. I was sixteen and heartbroken before he reminded me what it was like to laugh," he gripped his bottom lip into his mouth as I looked at him, pausing to think.

"Every good summer I have reminds me a lot of that one. This one is going to be a good one, I can tell, but I am not so naive, anymore. My spirit is less free. The buzzing planes overhead remind me of sitting on my grandma's porch in Cupertino and working at the animal shelter with him next to the private airport. All day small jet engines would pop from over the mountain ranges surrounding us and descend towards us slowly, passing twenty feet above us and haphazardly sputtering to a stop on the hot tarmac. The dogs vocal chords would rupture expectedly with an enthusiasm that made me panic. From the other end of the kennel he would yell something to me. Something comforting, I always liked that and never noticed."

He looked down at me, laughing as he started to say, "When I got my license, we planned on running away. Maine was our goal. As far from California as we could get. We made it to Arizona, to visit his friend in rehab. 'Why'd you relapse?' he had asked. His response: 'I like Lavocaine.' After that we were being followed by the police, so we hopped the border into Mexico. After that, I don't know. He led me so far away from myself. I don't know if I can forgive him for that. Even worse, I can't forget how well I got to know the side of myself he brought out."

"Where is he, now?" I asked.

"They say he'll be coming around again. I wonder what he'll be like. More than anything, I compare what I am now to what he probably is now. Has he made as many mistakes? Does he still hate himself? I know we won't have the same belly laughs because now we're filled with too many judgements and reservations. And if he still is anything like me, too much of us is left unshared. But we're old souls that know how to enjoy the retirement of youth."

I laughed at the simplicity of that, relieved for his ability to see the beauty in the small parts of the whole.

"For now, I want to hold onto these fleeting feelings and perhaps reminisce on those that have slipped away from me."

He quickly said, "So what's your reason for being out here?"

"I would tell you, but-"

He smiled and said, "But? The story of a guy getting a horse to ride around the coast isn't one I hear often."

"We're here," I said as I swept my arm towards the loose dirt of the road he was about to be on.

He smiled out of one side of his mouth and said, "So I won't ever get to know?"

"Afraid not," I told him.

"At least," he said, "I'll be free," he held up his hands.

I shook my head and cut the bindings on his wrists. I blinked, thinking of what I had to say, and smiled, hoping I could do it well. "I didn't want to impose on you too much. I hope I did the best I could."

"I think you did."

"Go down that road," I told him, "until you reach a farm. You mentioned that you have heard of Lavocaine, wiling to work with it?"

He smiled, "I've been to the towns."

"The what?" I asked as I helped him down. I hooked my foot into the stirrup and got into the saddle, backing White Stripe away from him as I did.

"To use Lavocaine you have to check into a designated town and do it there. You have to know about that, how do you not?"

"They never told me about that when I was there. By the way, you never told me your name," I said, holding down one eyebrow in a look of speculation.

"Nycho," he dipped his head with a smile as he told me.

"Fine, then you won't get my real name," I said.

He raised his face, "No, it is, I was named that."

"Well, I'm Ashna."

"Don't be like that," he said.

I grinned, "No, really, it is."

He smiled, then raised his brow, "By the way," I was about to turn away, but I looked at him as he said, "thanks for what you did. You didn't have to."

"Hey," I said, "good luck to you and your girlfriend. I wish the world for her."

He ducked his head under a hand, "Thanks, that means a lot." I watched him stretch out his legs and climb the remainder of the hill, then begin the endeavor down the road.

People are not concerned with the things that will kill them, as long as they make them look or feel good. If something has the propensity to kill them, then, they almost like it more, like they all want to be dead, anyway. If something takes a bit of work and will never kill you, nobody's interested in that. People are very averse to the things that'll make them look bad while they're alive. It seemed that the contributions to the world that people actually used were ones that kept killing them.

White Stripe and I hooked down the hill and back onto the highway. I used the guardrail on the right shoulder to protect us from cars as we meandered next to the cliffs and water. The roads twisted and sometimes turned into much less than two-lanes, but White Stripe and I kept our wits about us as we meandered south.

I idly thought about the reasons things were happening in this world. They were not necessarily opposite or antithetical to the world I had grownup in, but in so few ways was it identical that I could not convince myself that it was indeed the world I had always known. Perhaps the it was a purposive change or one that coincided with some pattern or design from before.

As I tried to explain away the world I was living in to myself, I remembered something I had noticed about people. People tend to reject coincidental explanations for things unless they have had some sort of indoctrination or beliefs inculcated in them by someone.

I thought of the perfectionist fallacy: if something is not perfect, it is not acceptable. Had I found the real world so unacceptable that I had turned it into one of contradictions? Had I believed that I could change it, a very blatant contradiction to what I knew about the real world?

I could completely lose myself in fantasies and theories, but when my exact desire are presented in front of me, I will put my hands up and hope not to receive it. I can fantasize for days about talking to a man on the phone, but were he to ask to have such a romantic conversation, I would refuse his request with some outstanding reason why I could not.

If someone were to come to me and White Stripe and ask if I would like to know why the world was such a changed one, I would smile and give them a superlative reason why I would rather keep on thinking about it.

CHAPTER TEN

The state's coastal arterial road pumped us into a small town of 500 people with a main road that pitched down into their town, then jutted out to a narrow pier. The town was a basin among low hills, a bowl that pooled out into a round bay, flanked on both sides by land that curved in on it to make a naturally occurring harbor.

I got off of White Stripe and took the backroads of the town, ever aware of people eyeing us as we peeked our heads around corners. Realizing nobody was against us being there, I walked him onto the town's main road, which made us face the ocean as we walked it. As we detoured into it I saw that the cliffs hugged around the water, town, and pier in a crescent. The town was nestled in between rolling hills, green undulations above the linear streets and buildings. People asked me my horse's name and offered him their hands to pet and sniff. To the first person that asked to pet White Stripe, I asked the name of the town.

"Arena Point, where are you from?" they said.

"Just a little bit south of here," I told them, walking on and watching the scope of view in front of me.

The water lapped past rock spears jutting from the ocean and entered, along with small boats, in between them in the afternoon light streaming from the sun as it persevered towards the water. A pier jutted out at the basin of the town, where the asphalt road abruptly met pebbly beach and the gray wood of the pier, with its few square bait and tackle shops plastered on it like barnacles. As we approached closer, I could hear the receding waves washing over the pebbles that carpeted the shore.

I saw that two lofty land masses hugged the water below them, forming an arena-like cove. The golden, rocky cliffs soared, then banked to make a sharp angle into grassy headlands. On one of the long, curving, crescent jetties, there sat their white and narrow lighthouse. I looked at it, far from us and thought of pushing my feet into White Stripe's belly and having him take us to it.

Abruptly, and very quickly, White Stripe and I both began to move together.

When you ride a horse, their gate is the first to move, then you do. Your movement and the horse's have a causal relationship. The walk usually sends you side to side, their trot forces you up and down, their canter back and forth, and gallop all four ways, almost at once, while the horse is moving at relative speeds. But this time he was not moving forward, but we were going every direction at once.

"We feel these every so often," yelled a woman near me. She yelled out, again, "Earthquake."

I was a California local and knew what an earthquake was when I felt one. I did not know, though, that they could happen so often. Could I began to look at her with widened eyes.

"Don't worry!" She yelled.

I looked around speculatively. The shaking was making innumerable objects clink together and the noise was immense.

"These buildings are very strong. This place is built on a fault," she said and she laughed. "You look like you're a tourist on the off-season with that dumb look."

I closed my mouth and she began walking. She passed into a doorway of a house completely surrounded with buoys for crab pots, fishing nets, and divers. I looked around the area, seeing the small houses leading to the pier and the cliffs leading to the crescent headlands on either side. The water came in through the small opening and was circled by the land. She came back out with a cup of coffee.

"Why are you on that horse?"

I felt my throat clench. Where you have a strong emotion, there will be attempts by others to use that to change your mind in a marketplace of interests, and something about her worried me.

"Adventure," I said off-handedly.

"Oh," she looked toward the crescent jetty and asked, "you work out?"

"Uh," I realized I had not stopped being shy and faltered with a response.

"No- I mean, do you swim?"

"Uh."

"Are you a good swimmer?" she asked.

My eyes scanned the choppy sea, measuring the enormity of it against the singularity of myself. I imagined what it was like when I had swum with my mother. I did not have many memories of her while she was alive that I was surprised I had not thought of this one before. I had been a very little girl, swimming beside my mom underwater in the sapphire haze of a swimming pool. I had looked at her, the burning of the pool's water a small price for the image of her next to me. I had felt like a whale calf with its mother, safe from danger, as I sidled next to her and we pushed our feet, hands against our sides.

I wanted my mother's protection, but knew I wouldn't find it. I was the age to start giving it to others, not taking it.

I stopped faltering with words and said, "Never had a problem."

The earthquake become more mild, she smiled something that looked like relief, and said, "There's a feisty old man that just lost one of his divers up there," her eyes wandered up the cliff. "It looks like you just got to town." It was a statement, but her quizzical look made it a query, "Don't have a job? He pays good money if you make him good money," she said. "Well, anyway, start getting used to these earthquakes, we have about a hundred a day. Take this, for now," she handed me a sandwich wrapped in a paper towel.

"Well," I faltered with words, "thank you."

"Anytime," she said and began to withdraw into her adorned house.

"Wait," I called out, "you said that you're on a fault line, what's it called?"

"Anna Saders," she shouted back as she receded into her house.

"Of course," I told White Stripe as we turned to canter up the hill out onto one of the crescent jetties.

I thought of the perfectionist fallacy: if something is not perfect, it is not acceptable. Had I found the real world so unacceptable that I had turned it into one of contradictions? Had I believed that I could change it, a very blatant contradiction to what I knew about the real world?

A fishing line caught my attention, it was cast a great distance and my eyes couldn't help but track it to the lapping water as it ebbed and flowed. The roar of noise as its azure blue spit covered rocks, frothing over them, reached my ears from the many hundreds of feet between us.

I quickly tried to gauge the fisherman as I registered another earthquake, less perceptible now that I was west of the shoreline, and dismounted White Stripe as he was taking it in stride by pacing tangentially around. I reined him in and patted him down as I approached the fisherman.

"Don't let the horse go!" He yelled over to me. A burst of wind caught my face with the ocean's deep, layered, musky slap. I shook my head sideways, blowing out my nose. White Stripe probably got the same whiff and snotted out. When they're annoyed, horses sometimes shake, a little like a dog shaking off water, but with ten to the power of four the amount of mass behind it. He did that here, his body sparkling as the dust and skin particles that he had expelled were able to catch the light before they drifted away.

"No, I won't. We've both had an enjoyable day and," I looked at White Stripe as he shuffled, cautiously as the earthquake had worsened, toward me, "we wouldn't want to leave each other's company just yet."

"Good enough, well what are you doing up here? Maybe you should leave!" He yelled.

I said, "Woh, man!" Like I was some kind of jackass that couldn't understand invasion of privacy or space.

"This ground doesn't have dense root systems. Just this bloody stuff," he kicked green chunks of grass from the ground to the air and away from his chair, which had three lunch-pails and one small canteen next to where his green flip-flop outfitted feet were. He was wearing an extra large jacket with the sleeves rolled up to expose very small forearms and knee-length shorts.

"Oh," I said, not understanding.

"Your horse is too heavy!" He yelled.

I felt a blush rise to my cheeks and I half bowed as I waved and walked away.

White Stripe had stifled breathing as we found a more inland part of the headlands for me to open the saddlebag and latch his halter to a lead and a stake in the ground.

I ran back to the fisherman, thinking before I reached him and said, "A lady in town told me to meet you up here."

"Makes sense," he nodded as he spoke, leaning back and smiling widely. "Are you a strong swimmer?"

"I am," I said.

"Then we'll go diving! Tonight." He spoke cryptically, "Tell no one. Bowling ball beach. Meet me again."

I nodded to him and half-bowed, probably because he was a solid Asian man with a face that asked for respect and dignity. I reminded myself not to impose my desires, and that meant not to become stifling to others by mis-understanding their cultures.

He sat nonchalantly and I ran back to White Stripe, getting the stake out of the ground and in the bag, just as another earthquake hit.

"They have to be a consistent time apart, huh, White Stripe?" He bowed his head to his foreleg and nuzzled an itch as I continued, "Let me get this off of you," as I unlatched the saddlebags and slung them on one shoulder, "so that I can lead you somewhere and brush you down, eh?" I asked him with an intonation of hope and worry. He looked at me with a tired, sunken in expression.

"I shouldn't have ridden you so hard the first day out, huh?" I asked as I led him back east on the headlands where I could walk him in the taller grass. When we got there, I took his saddle off, I let him browse the selection of grasses. Another earthquake shook me until I had to stand up and stretch my legs as I looked around at the trees above us. I rummaged in the saddlebag, "There must be some pattern," I said to the bag and myself.

I looked over to White Stripe and realized he had enough of a sweat to warrant taking all of his tack off and rubbing a curry comb to his flank. Delicately, I removed the sticky sweat with that and a boar-hair brush. I put my bag under his saddle and laid down to let him graze and for me to nap off the day's trek south. I let the sun slide down the hot sky, like an egg yolk in a greased frying pan. Melting like solid butter into bubbling grease, I let the sun warm my body until I was dozing.

He tugged on the rope after the sun had thoroughly warmed me. I decided to get up and gaze over the side of the cliff. Like most of the cliffs, this one had a near-vertical drop and its face extended for hundreds of feet. Wind propped me up as I peered over the edge. I led White Stripe away from the unstable side of the cliff and put the saddle and bags on him, cinching it up fully.

"I'll tell you, White Stripe, I cinch the girth up all the way and then some," as I latched the metal through the leather hole near the top of the strap, I said, "If this was too loose, the saddle could go sliding to the side and bring my butt to your belly." Memories danced at the edge of my vision, but I smiled and talked over them, "The thing to remember about falling off a horse is to pull your tongue in, but the hardest part about falling off a horse is getting stuck in between its hooves. You don't always get back up right away."

I adjusted the stirrups back from the galloping position by lowering them a few notches, but continued to talk about cinching the girth, "If you blow out your belly to make it bigger when I cinch it on, it could be too loose and the saddle would slip out under me. If I didn't get my feet out of there, I would be dangling between these bad guys," I said as I ran a hand down his shoulder, to his leg, then to the others. I inspected his hooves, making sure he hadn't gotten too many rocks and dirt in them during the gallop. I patted his back when I was done, proud of his worthwhile effort, and sat down.

White Stripe pricked his ears and stopped eating grass to swerve his head toward me. From the ground, he looked like a long-neck dinosaur. His velvet-soft nose nuzzled into my chest and he rubbed his eye next to my cheek. I could feel the wet goop of his eye staining my skin. His breathe was powerful, blowing my clothing like ruffled feathers of a bird, before he pulled away rather abruptly. He touched the ground close to me with his lips, then turned to eat somewhere else.

I looked around as a series of earthquake tremors began, White Stripe took two steps to the side and I said, "Don't side-step, now, boy."

I knew I needed to find him a place to be stalled up for the night and began taking him back into town. The lady that had been outside of her buoyed home was walking along the town's pier entrance when I got there. White Stripe heard the hollow sound of his hooves against only wood as we walked onto the pier's octagonal entry and backed back onto concrete.

"You're one needy man," came the woman's voice.

I turned to her, ashamed, "I am, I'll be needing to put him up somewhere." I said.

"You'll need to go where it's zoned for your horse," she told me, clasping her hands.

I said, "Shoot, well we are mobile."

"What about yourself?" She asked, "Will you be needing to be put up somewhere?"

Something foreign in me pulsed, like the flow of blood to it had only just been un-dammed as I said, "I would only be willing with the likes of you," with a stutter.

"Well you are a lucky man, too," as she turned as both and had us follow her back to her house, "I was given this Inn by some family."

"Put your things in here and I'll point you toward my house on the edge of town. It's got a fenced-in yard. I hope it'll work. My dog should be inside, but he won't be too much trouble. Take down the laundry line, you know," she pointed to White Stripe.

We trotted that way and the address matched the one she had etched into my hand. I looked from the scrawled black lines on my hand to the red block numbers on the sky-blue mailbox, whose post had vining green plants straddling it vertically. I tugged on the string on top of the gate and it swung open. White Stripe followed me in and I found the grassy backyard was well fenced. I took his saddle, bags, and bridle up to a railing and set them there. Another earthquake began as White Stripe raised his head and pricked his ears toward the eastern mountains.

"Woh, now, pony," I called out words that soothed him and he snorted as he bent back down to chew the grass.

I walked myself back through town, bemusing myself by watching the flags from poles rumple in the wind and release themselves back out, according to the will of the wind. My legs ached and I walked bow-legged, but the people didn't seem to notice as they smiled and waved, some asking if they had seen me on a horse.

The woman was outside of her cluttered Inn, watching the sunset. Her curly hair was picked up by the wind, then settled on her shoulders again, like the flags being raised without their will.

She turned at my approach, smiling sweetly, "I didn't catch your name," she said.

I said, "I didn't give it, I'm Ashna."

"Beautiful name," she said.

"And you are?" I asked.

"Aurora," she said simply.

"Last name, borealis?" I asked.

She laughed, "I'm not that special."

I said, "Maybe you are."

She put a hand on my chest, her fingers soft against the hard, linear plane there, "I don't think so," she said as she lifted her hand and looked away. I ruminated on what I had gone through in the last month. I was not so special when the rest of the world could be flipped on its axis.

"The fisherman will want to see you, come back to my house for some warm food and a warmer bed when you're all done," she said and I nodded before leaving.

CHAPTER ELEVEN

The climb up the hill was steeper without a horse and I felt my palms press against my thighs like I had done when climbing up from the stream I had skinny dipped in before meeting White Stripe and Robert.

The man was not there. I sunk into a despair as the cold ocean wind came in and the earth trembled. Something in my memory tingled and I remembered hearing him say, "Bowling ball beach."

I turned myself away from the pier and the other, distant, crescent jetty and skipped quickly down the grassy headlands to find myself on a rocky trail that curved down bluffs. Sand scattered from under my feet and I jumped onto ledges, almost unaware of where my feet were taking me.

As I found myself at sea level, another earthquake began and the moon's three-quarter glow was the only light, save the stars. With shaky legs I began to walk, picking my eyes up from the ground near me to see an enduring red gleam on the beach, perturbed only by large, bowling ball-like spheres of rock.

I gasped, looking around myself. Nothing was illuminated but the beach, with its phosphorescent glow trailing along the waterline. The rosy globs and dots radiated from the places along the water where they were propelled from the water to the sandy beach. There, on the beach, were lines of balls, their black forms visible as they were silhouetted by the crimson glow behind them.

Despite the earthquake, I ran forward to where the first rocky globes began. They were thigh-height and set in rows. If I had had more light, I thought I could count, then multiply the number of balls in the two bisecting lines to find out how many there were. But in the dark of the night I only saw those directly around me and those illuminated by the red glow that were closer to the water. I touched one as it trembled with the earth, my fingers gliding around its rippled surface. The sea breeze had licked the undulating surface of them and left them wet and cold to the touch.

I thought I could understand how the constant earthquakes could form these cannonball formations, but my mind ran circles, knowing I really couldn't do anything but theorize. I stood more fully to walk toward the twinkling scarlet lights on the rocks closer to the water, upset knowing that whatever I saw in those would only be theoretical, too.

As I stood, I heard a shout, "Ayo!" I stopped moving and looked around, seeing at first nothing, before my eyes settled on a waving light of a headlamp as it glided down the same pass I had come through. The light approached and I recognized the fisherman as he took off the headlamp and handed it to me to use. He smiled enthusiastically as he pulled one out of his jacket pocket, untwisting the nylon band and strapping it to his head.

"Waterproof!" He exclaimed simply, pointing to both of our lights.

"Good..." I said, wondering what it was good for.

"Have you ever dove before?" He asked, quickly walking towards the glow next to the water's edge.

I walked next to him, my fingers tingling, saying, "I used to swim down, reaching out my arm, trying to feel the bottom of the ponds or pools with my fingers. I didn't get good at it," I smiled, "but I liked it." I could barely hear my own words over the sound of the rushing waves. I looked towards the ocean, thinking of Kate Chopin writing that the ocean's, "...sonorous murmur reached her like a loving but imperative entreaty," as the rolling tide brought with it a calming that only it could provide. I sighed into it, forgetting past regrets and mistakes, seeing only the ocean.

He chuckled, "That is good," then bent down, shifting the weight of the duffel bag he was carrying, as he did. He picked up some of the red, radiant luminescence I had seen. He moved his fingers and it moved sporadically around in his palm. I saw the lines of his hands under the water and fiery red orbs crease against one another. Some of the pin-drop sized lights blinked ephemerally then extinguished for good, while others simply dimmed only to regain their gleam.

"Algae," he said, smiling, "phosphorescent algae."

"I thought it was just another trick of this crazy world you live in," I said and he laughed like he understood. Maybe he didn't or maybe he knew more than me. He nodded to me and dropped the contents of his hand into mine. I smiled as I took it and poked at the phosphorescent algae.

"Not a good night for fishing," he said as he continued to walk adjacent to the water.

My heart sank, "Why?" I had been asked to fish and now I was simply walking around some bioluminescence and shaking balls.

"These," he pointed at the clusters of wine-colored spherules, "require energy to light up. When there is movement in the water, they get that energy and a trail lights in the movement's path. It is bright red where you have been, where you are, all of the places you've displaced water."

I said dejectedly, "Oh."

"But," his voice became shrill and I looked at him as he spoke with zest, "great for diving for things that I bet you have never seen before." He smiled widely and I did, too, as I continued the walk with him. We approached a jutting of black rocks, their presence seemed to upset the ocean as it battered and beat the rocks, only relenting to gather itself back to push again, against the sharpened rocks.

"Heehee," giggled the fisherman as he set the bag on a tall ledge. I looked at him, daunted by the idea of the task.

"Take it all off!" He barked at me, throwing a finger up and down, pointing flippantly at my clothes. I immediately felt a blush, a concern, a lack for words. That embarrassment was halted as I felt my penis retract into my body. I wasn't a woman and I didn't need to keep a guard up to protect my body anymore. I exhaled and he told me again to undress. The cold was pushing against my jacket and jeans anyway, it made only the slightest difference. I pulled off each article of clothing and he took them, rolling them up and putting them in his bag as he pulled out a black mass. He unfolded it and I realized it was a wetsuit.

"Those too," he said, pointing at my boxers gruffly.

I looked down, past the empty place where my buoyant breasts had once been. My hands fluttered to the place they were once, now empty and devoid of the resplendence. I lowered my hands and pulled, then pushed, then released the elastic of my boxers. Huddled up to my skin like a cold, scared child, my penis was exposed now.

The fisherman did not stare at it as I did, but handed me the wetsuit and busied himself in the duffel. I pulled it over my feet and legs, like I had done when I had worn tights. The air from the sea caught on a tear wobbling on the edge of my lid and made the trail it left on my skin colder than the rest of my face. I let another tear fall and wiped my face, content to let a sadness bury itself in me without taking the time to understand it. I pulled the wetsuit over half of my torso and put my arms in, feeling like meat encased in a thin wrapper.

The fisherman looked up, nodding and turning his finger for me to show him my back. I turned and he zipped the clunky plastic zipper, pulling as it paused between my shoulders, until it was fully encasing me, from my ankles to my neck.

He smiled and dug into the bag, then with both hands he showed me a shell. "Do you know what this is?"

I said, "An oyster."

He smiled sweetly, "Yes," and shone his headlamp onto it. Its outer edges were dull and lumpy, like layers of gray earth, and it looked unappealing. Like a locket, he opened it to reveal that it was empty, as if there was no picture worthy to fill it.

He told me, "This is what you will find."

I asked, "Only one?"

"Many!" He said, with a laugh, and handed me a large belt with a thick plastic clip. He attached a drawstring bag to one side and a knife holster to the other. I looked at him. He wasn't wearing a wetsuit, but a skimpy speedo that didn't hide the curving lines of his lower abdomen muscles that led up to a round, full belly. He zipped up the duffel and positioned it securely on the ledge.

"Follow," he said loudly over the pounding of the surf. As he planted his feet in niches of rock and water, I followed, climbing haphazardly as we made the ascent together. We sidled along the rock, making our way to the place where the rock curved and began to form the inner part of the southern crescent jetty. When we were hundreds of feet west of the beach we had come from, the glittering of the vermilion algae as it was pushed onto the beach looked like one large maroon specter. He raised a fist and I halted.

"This is good. Do not let the ocean pull you, but pull the ocean." I looked at him, hoping the wisdom was only the first bucket from the well, but he spoke no more.

"I should go in here," I said, hoping he would shake his head, no. He nodded a yes, pleasantly smiling.

"I should dive down to get oysters," I said, looking at the water ebbing and pooling against the rock-face, "here."

He nodded, bending his knees and balancing on the balls of his feet. He looked at the water, too, smiling. The moon cast no shadows now as it grew even brighter. I picked the placement of my feet carefully. The water embraced my toes and quelled the burning sensation from walking on the sharp rocks. It moved up my leg without me moving in deeper and I thought about taking the first step in a run. The only thing to do was decide to do something and follow through with it. I lunged forward, embracing the movement of the water around me before moving with it. I swept my arms out and propelled forward, scanning the water with the headlight for any obstacles. I threw my hands in front of me, then pulled them to my sides, swimming deeper. I kicked my feet and stroked with my hands until I was deep enough to the rocks. My lungs panicked, making me look up at the churning surface thirty feet above me. Seeing the cherry trail of glowing algae I had left as I had moved made me look back down, intent on reaching the bottom.

I forced my hands to push me closer to a rocky outcropping. I held onto it with one hand and thrust myself up and down, pushing my fingers to feel and pull on every crevice. My hand moved faster than my mind as it bolted to hold up what, at first glance, looked like an oyster. I dropped it quickly as I realized it was a rock. My head bobbed up and down, searching. After only seconds I shook my head, about to kick the water with both feet and shoot back to the surface, before a dull gray lip caught my eye. I tried to pick it up but it wouldn't move. My vision quivered as my arms' muscles worked to pry it from the rock shelf. I thought of my knife and, with one hand latched to the oyster, I unclipped it from the belt. Without removing it from the holster, I banged it against the joint between the oyster and the rock, it loosened and when it detached, I floated up.

Happily, I kicked my feet and carefully surfaced. My headlight shone on the fisherman's face almost immediately. I held up both hands.

"Put it in your bag!" He shouted. I looked down, frowning at my hip belt under the water as I loosened the drawstring and dropped the cloudy oyster in.

"Good! Again!" He yelled and I clipped my knife back in before curling my torso and sinking back into the water. The churning water pushed me away from the rock from which a glittering ruby trail of single-celled bioluminescent algae glowed. I tugged at rocks and sea grass, exposing an outcropping of three dingy gray oysters. I pried two out before my lungs burned so fiercely that I let my buoyancy bring me back to the surface. When I surfaced the fisherman just smiled hopefully, then I dove back down to the third one I couldn't get. I searched around the area but there were none to be found. I surfaced, dove, surfaced, and dove four times before finding another.

Over the pounding waves' noise I told the fisherman, "I have four!"

He only said, "More!" I nodded and dove again, kicking my feet like seal flippers, twisting and contouring my body, relaxing it when I wanted to surface. I melded with the water, only occasionally finding myself knocking against rocks or kicking them unintentionally.

I spotted deeper places, diving more than forty feet, finding the two biggest oysters I had ever seen in an eel hole. I removed them quickly, disconcerted by a potential and mysterious threat. When I surfaced after them, he ushered me up with a sweeping of his hand toward him in the harsh light of his own headlamp.

While the water was flowing toward him, I pulled my legs up as my palms pushed against the rock. He offered a hand and I took it, grateful. He unclipped my belt for me and put it around his waist. He pointed his hands, then launched from the rocks into the water. I watched as his light grew increasingly distant and murky. Then as it shot toward me a few minutes later. I only heard him gasp in air and splash back down, his ethereal light followed by a dim trail of tiny glowing scarlet orbs. I watched him as he had watched me. The ocean was growing choppy and I was growing nervous. He was down longer than I thought possible. When his light turned towards the surface, I grew relieved and found I had been holding my breathe with him as I sighed.

After he dove for what seemed like ten times longer than me, he pulled himself to sit next to me and said, "Now you." The belt felt much heavier when I put it on and it acted as a weight. I had more time on the bottom because of it and added at least five more to the bag before he ushered me out, again. I relaxed as I kneeled, watching the stars blinking their white lights as the once-vibrant moon faded behind a navy veil of night.

Gravity bends light, but because it does, that means clocks that are closer to the center of the earth move slower. For the same reason, time moves slower next to a black hole. Like gravity, work seemed to slow time, to hold me away from my own aging and demise. Working ceaselessly, starting without questioning, and not stopping felt as freeing from the burdens of time as gravity.

I watched the fisherman's moon-like glow of his headlight as it approached the surface, then looked away as he surfaced and handed off the belt. I submerged my body, feeling the crushing weight of the ocean both pulling and pushing me. My hands knew their roles now as the left held tightly to the oysters, the tips growing raw and burning with the repetition, and my right used leverage to scrape them from their moorings.

A particular oyster, more pink than grey, with lines of red embedded on the shell, caught my finger in its lip. I watched the red of my blood turn greenish as it floated away. My eyes stung, like hundreds of paper cuts all at once. I decided to return to the surface and stuffed the oyster into the brimming bag. The drawstring didn't pull tight and a small bit of the red oyster peaked out from the top. Carefully blinking, I swam up and pulled myself to stand next to the fisherman.

He smiled giddily as he realized the bag was too full to keep going. We picked our way back to the beginning of the beach, where he quickly shed his speedo and replaced it with long pants and a sweatshirt. I put the belt in his duffel and took out my own clothes after peeling off the wetsuit. My body was relatively dry for being in the water so long, but water ran rivers down my body from my hair and my instincts told me to throw all of my clothes on as quickly as I could, resulting in sand strewn to every far-flung region of my body. I was warmer than before, no longer gripped on all sides by icy wind nor water, and bounced on the balls of my feet.

The fisherman grabbed from his duffel pants and pushed his ankle high in the air in order to put it through a leg of them, then did so with the next. He sat next to his bag and began taking out tools to open the oysters while saying, "Come again tomorrow and I will pay you."

"Where," I asked, "here?"

"No, no," he said, delicately scraping the inside of the oyster with a rod, "Up on- oh!" He stopped speaking to raise his oyster, the pink one that had been on top, above his head before yelling loudly and lifting his legs up from the ground. He began dancing and I picked up the headlamp, clicking it on, to point it at his hands. Between two fingers of one hand was a pearl, larger than his eye. He waved it in the air and bellowed at the sea. I wondered how many of them were in the bag, and looked at it speculatively.

He remembered my presence and said, "Ayo! You, look!"

He placed the pearl under my vision and I noticed its perfection, feigning impression with a soft, "Wow."

"You do not understand," he said, bitterly withdrawing the pearl from my vision.

"What can you do with that?" I asked. He stroked it, then slowly slipped it into his pant's pocket. He remained fixated on not speaking.

He picked up a new oyster to study it, then pried it open and said, "Two things with that one. Two very important things." He threw the small pearl in the bag and yelled, "Not jewelry!" He performed the same action of putting a vice grip around the bivalve of the next oyster, quickly jerking his rod in, then out as an irregularly shaped pearl dropped into his hand.

"Marriage ceremony," he said, "or stomach medicine for this one. You want to eat it?" His hand outstretched towards my mouth with the pearl, "Or back in the ocean for the fish." He threw his hand back behind his back, but I saw him drop it into his other pant's pocket. Then, as if he hadn't been hooting and hollering moments ago, he began steadily prying open the next oyster.

"You are out very late," he said.

"No later than I normally stay up."

"Really?" he asked.

"Oh yeah."

"Most people are asleep before the sun sets. You do not do this," he said as he picked through the bag and found pearls.

It was my turn to ask, "Really?"

"Oh yes," he said, "definitely."

"How late do they sleep in?"

"They never wake up before noon."

"What about you?"

"I am not of this world," he said, erupting in laughter.

"Neither am I."

He stood for a moment, motionless, staring at me, then said, "It is not so easy to tell. Bah! Away with you, whoever you are."

I walked up the bluff, gripping things I couldn't see, stumbling over rocks, and misguiding myself. The wind on the top of the headlands whipped at my hair and clothes and the air hurt my face, but I persevered to the town, walking through the empty streets, embodying the lone wolf. Happily strung were twinkling lights and banners, distinctly different from the narrow and forlorn lone wolf I saw in myself.

There was no cure for this, it would follow me for the rest of my life. There was no gift to change it. There was no happiness to engulf me, nothing to uplift me and help me keep my head. There was no definite way to alleviate the entrappings of the spirit that lay in me, wild and tired of all that was and would come. All that I had to appease my hunger for something different and new was my self.

I did not want my heart to be a hunter. I did not want men and women to walk past me and feel like they are my prey. And so, I walked in solitude, hoping to be an idealistic, moral servant to the world and feel at once wise and more righteous for it. I could see beauty in the physical mirror, seeing it in the metaphorical mirror of the world is what I strived for. I wore lenses that kept everyone at a distance, for so long I had, that they had made fissions. It was my perception of beauty that was skewed, not the world's inability at being beautiful.

In the growing evening there was humane warmth and it relaxed my shoulders. I swung an arm up from beside my hip to bend back, then let it fall. I studied the town, it's sporadic cobblestone alleys and shining, freshly painted storefronts. Pastels of different hues and the same colors gleamed from the walls and little bunting flags waved across the windows and some doorways. My shirt had shifted and as I went to correct it, my nose alighted with the beckoningly fresh, sugared scent of gardenias that, with no frivolity, threw their scents into the night. Uninhibited and purely strung out on the scent, I leaned my head over my shoulder to allow the scent ingress to me.

I recalled an old lesson I had taught myself. It was to be proud of who you are and never ashamed of how you came to find out. I raised my arms to allow my palms to be level with my shoulders as I walked, smiling as I swayed my hips and pushed my legs down the street.

The redolent fragrance of sweet gardenias was a strong reminder of days in my backyard as a young girl, bent over books as the sun, insects, and winds moved above me. The themes, plots, and problems that appeared at-once in my eyes, then my mind, taught me what to be aware of when living my life and how to do it to the fullest. I had fallen, I had stumbled, I had been put in compromising situations, but the books had given me confidence. The books had told me what could happen and what to do. If I were to be proud of anything, it would be that I lived in a world where the written word existed.

I let my hands settle behind my back, trusting the street as I leaned my head up and watched the sky turn murky with stars. The town's frontages pushed me through and I thought of those long days as a child, and how they had led here. Since I had begun aging, I had grown more and more fearful of remaining the same. Perhaps it was my main fear to stay some way that I hate, forever, that persistently forced me to develop and grow. I was thankful every day that I was able to change or become something new that I enjoyed. And thankful, too, for every time that I changed back to some earlier way I had been after developing in some manner that I did not enjoy.

Perhaps that was why I had developed a fictive incarnation of my self. It is something to go back to. It is the constant in my experiment. It is what will not change. Because, what can change a lone wolf, after all, but the lone wolf?

I tucked my chin next to my neck and looked straight ahead, wondering if I would tell myself the answer. I though of Lane, with her pretty hair and prettier eyes. Her one in a billion blood with all of its helixes. Her mind. That's what kept me. That's what shackled me to consistency and regularity.

She had loved me until my stories bled ink, not blood.

I had transferred all of that love into myself. I had woken up and found I didn't need to love her. It was funny how quickly and independently my mind can work from my heart. Without even wanting to, I had no need to know her. No need but to know myself, a vessel that was already brimming and perhaps only wanted her as a place to spill out into.

I stepped with pride and pleasure, feeling each stride a testament to my castration from the throes of fraternity and society. I isolated myself by always moving, and as I walked through the town I planned the way I could remove myself from them further. I made a blueprint in my brain of the places and terrain I would throw myself over next, knowing that before I could, I had to sleep. The need for rest jostled my withdrawn and self-affectionate thoughts into the back of my mind as I sauntered towards Aurora's house.

Chapter twelve

When I reached Aurora's house, I opened the back gate and heard White Stripe's low nicker. "Hey boy," I said and I heard his hooves hitting turf toward me. I put a hand on the white stripe on his face and buried my other hand in his hair. I inhaled, feeling the smell of him in my nose, settling back into my skin.

A light flicked on and Aurora was at her porch doorway. I looked at her happily, she was kind and sweet, but not a bit undesirable. I felt the pump of blood spur my groin and I looked away.

"I put a blanket on him," she said smoothly.

"You what?" I asked.

She laughed softly, then said, "You're looking right at it."

I gave a short laugh and ran my hands through my damp hair a few times, "So you did. Thank you." I walked past him, patting the thick blanket she had put on him, and ascended her deck stairs.

"You're a mess," she said as I got close, sweeping my hair into her hand and squeezing it into her other hand. She retracted her palm, then flung the water off of it, onto the porch. Her lips curved into a smile, replacing the concern etched there, and beckoned me into the house. A corgi ran up to me, its entire body bopping towards me and from me. I tried to put a hand out to him and he just ran away, thumping up the stairs.

Without willing myself to, I was watching her move. My eyes swept across her body like I was reading lines of a newspaper and they settled on the pictures. I read her like an advertisement and shame forced blood throughout my body. I was so confused, my body didn't know if it should send blood to my cheeks or my penis, so it did both.

"Shower should get hot pretty quickly. You don't seem the sort of man that needs a cold shower," she said wryly, pointing to a bathroom as she passed me through her hallway, "so give it a minute before getting in. Do you want to eat something first?" I shook my head, concerned that she would witness the new arrival in my pants before I could slip off my clothes. She nodded quickly, then handed me a towel and was out of the hallway.

I walked into the bathroom and turned on the shower, hearing the knob squeak until the valve was fully open. The water pitter-pattered on the shower floor as I disrobed and looked down to see my fully erect penis.

I forgot about the heartaches of losing what I had once loved. I forgot about the confusion abounding over me on the state of this world. I forgot everything with the first touch of my hand to the soft skin.

It felt like warmth. It felt like nothing I had ever had. It felt like nothing I had ever known.

I looked around, pumping a bit of moisturizer from a tube into my hand. I let my hand glide across it, feeling the ripples and texture. Steam ebbed from the shower and became evanescent around me. I mixed slow rhythm with jerks of my wrist. I mixed fast pumps with gentle taps of my fingers. I mixed up who I was, thinking about the woman I had once been, thinking about the naive woman I had once been that didn't know how deliriously otherworldly it was to have this.

I paused in order to walk into the shower, groaning quietly as the water hit my back and I bent over, resting my forehead on the wall. Masturbation had felt like a dessert as a woman. As a man, it felt like all three meals. It was relief. It was everything I needed. It was done before I had really started.

For too long I let the water hit me until it turned cold, stifling my breathe and making me scrub my body quickly with my hands. Pellets of sand hit the shower floor and skittered away as I wiped crevices clean. Water slapped my hair and I jumped to turn the handle of the faucet, closing the tap.

When the shower was off, Aurora knocked on the door and said, "I left a towel for you on the seat and took some of your clothes out of the bags outside and put them there, too."

I said, "Very kind of you!"

I pushed it to my face and sighed relief.

"You hungry, love?" She asked from the hall as I felt the tremors of an earthquake begin.

Instinctually, I said, "No, not at all." Porcelain on the shelf stood still during the shaking. I delicately pulled on it and it wouldn't move from the shelf.

"I smell a lie," she laughed. "I already fixed you up something. Hurry up and come on out."

"Thank you!" I said. What a wonderful person, I thought as I shook my hair out, smiling at the bathroom tiles.

Before I left the bathroom, I wadded my dirty clothes up and carried them in the crook of my arm into the hallway. I padded on bare feet to the backdoor and had my hand on the handle when I heard Aurora's voice.

"Do you need laundry done?" She called out.

I smiled and yelled, "Maybe."

"Get some stuff together, then, and put them in a pile." She called, "Hurry it up before this gets cold. Not that they won't be good."

I tried to place the smell as I went outside to get my dirty clothes. She had put something in the oven, that was definite. It was sweet and buttery. I felt like I could smell the popping, sizzling sounds of it as it baked. I loaded my arms with clothes and she came out to take them, smiling sweetly and telling me she would meet me in the dining room.

I followed my nose and found myself sitting in front of a circle of white cheese, melting into greasy scalloped potatoes and broccoli. I dug one of the grainy crackers that fanned out around the creamy mound into the melted cheese, both relishing and not recognizing the taste on my palette.

Aurora stepped into the dining room and sat opposite of me, smiling as she pushed a cracker into the cheese and lifted it to her mouth.

"What kind of cheese is this?" I asked.

"Reblechon. It's good, isn't it? Use a fork to really get the vegetables," she said, picking up two and handing one to me. She was a beautiful woman with crow's feet and laugh lines that spoke more than she did. Her curly hair shook as she looked about and brushed her shoulders like a brush against canvas, creating delicate trails. I wanted to speak to her, but was ravished and ate hungrily, instead.

"Would you like some wine with this?"

She asked as a matter of courtesy, but I shook my head, "No, but thank you."

"Oh?" she said with the question she was suppressing furrowed into her brow.

I said, "I know I look more interesting," she creased the edges of her eyes as she listened, "but I'm simply not a drinker."

"Well, I want to know what makes you interesting. How long have you been traveling?"

"A month or so. Not long at all," I said, looking in her beautiful eyes. She spent a moment looking at me before speaking.

She said, "That's not too bad at all," making me wonder if their was a stigma she had about traveling.

"It's been a learning experience. Traveling alone can really show you the way the world doesn't make sense," I said.

"Well, it's good you're a man." She stated plainly, "It's not safe traveling alone if you're a girl."

"It's not safe to breathe alone if you're a girl, apparently," I said, bitterly.

She laughed, perhaps sensing my anger, and waved it away with her hand, "So where did you come from?"

I said, "I was at a University, then started working, then I fell in love," I recalled what it was like before White Stripe. To stop thinking about the love I had lost, I said, "I liked learning."

"What did you study?" She asked politely.

"All different things," I said ambiguously. "I studied humanities, sciences, philosophy, psychology, but it all doesn't matter, I suppose. I don't see myself completing anything that really alleviates the world's burdens."

She poured waters and asked, "What does that mean?"

"I just get so sad," I sighed and she nodded, "about the global crisis and the futility of trying at all."

"At least you're privileged enough to sit here and talk about it like this," she said.

"Not lucky enough to make a difference in the lives of people that aren't."

"I don't know about that," she said with both hope and despair etching the side of her mouth.

I said, "I may be wrong, but some young kid," I had almost called myself a girl instead of kid, "isn't going to change how the world looks at things."

"You have to work hard for what you want," she told me.

I struggled to contain words as I finished my mouthful of food, "I have!"

"You have to work hard for a very long time," she intoned.

I lifted my fork to my mouth and smiled, "Point taken. I don't know how long I can work without seeing that outcome."

She turned her head and her hands slid together, then pressed themselves between her thighs, "You don't really do it for the outcome, do you?"

"Keaton Henson said, 'I think a lot of art is trying to make someone love you.'"

"He may be right. Who is that?" she asked.

"Oh, a musician. Doesn't get out much, so he isn't very well known. An old girlfriend," I faltered with my fork, "told me about him." I looked up, partly penitent for having mentioned an old love, and saw her looking distantly at her house,

"I think I make art to bring people back."

I looked up, "Yes," I said, staring at the bundles of tears next to her eyelids, "I do, too."

Her words were cooly self-possessed as she said them, "Granted, there is an art to living."

I smiled, "I like to try to make my life a living piece of art with no public display or exhibition. Granted, I would be the main viewer, if ever there was one, but it seems I am the only one suited to it."

Like a piece of laundry flapping in the breeze, her smile found a place in the corners of her mouth, flickering there and moving down

She inhaled and smiled wearily, saying, "What did you do with Raluca?"

I felt like she was redirecting the conversation after taking too much of a mentor role in it, but had to ask, "Is Raluca the fisherman?" She nodded and I excitedly told her, "We went diving for oysters."

"Did he open any up?" She asked.

I thought of the big one, "Yes."

"Well?"

I said, "Incredible."

She shook her head, tight curls swaying, as she said, "He does amazing work."

I furrowed my brow as she took the remnants of what had been of the pan of reblechon and potatoes away, "What exactly?"

"Some of this some of that. With the mediocre pearls he'll perform Hindu marriage ceremonies. They will drill a hole into a virgin pearl on the day of the wedding. A beautiful event," she said as she stood next to me with the pan.

I thought of his whooping and hollering, asking, "And with the big ones?"

She reached for a chair with a free hand as another earthquake began, "Have you ever heard of the pearly gates?"

"I have," I said as she went into the kitchen.

She smiled as she came back into the room, "He makes those. He is truly a gift to the town."

I felt exhausted, "The what?"

She smiled, "The pearly gates into heaven."

I was shaking with words, "I don't believe in heaven."

She shrugged, "That's okay."

"But," I began to speak and she raised a hand.

She said, "Trust me and ask Raluca."

"That aside," I said as I played with a trinket on the table, "tell me, how long have you been here?"

She shrugged, "My whole life."

"That's phenomenal," I said.

She chuckled, "Is it? Like I said, I was bequeathed the inn you met me at. I don't like it as much as the tourists do."

I thought of the buoy-festooned inn, incomparable to her house in its ramshackle way. Her home was modest, cluttered but not over-filled. I was relaxed in it in a way that made me feel guilty for sullying it in any way. I smiled at it in appreciation, then began to wonder about her. I tried to study the pictures on the walls, finding no semblance between her and the people in them.

As the earthquake alleviated, I began to ask, "Aurora, do you have-"

She shook her head, "No, no. You know, some people can't have a family."

"I never thought about that," I said. Hairs raised on my neck and arms. My instincts told me it was too cold, then too hot. I took a deep breathe, breathing out the queasy understanding that I couldn't reproduce inside of myself as a man. With this penis came the lack of all of the organs I needed to continue on thinking about children coming into my life in a decade or two. It was no longer my choice, I had no control over it. If I ever wanted to, I would have to not only be with a woman whom I loved, but she would have to want it, too. What was in there, now, if not a bunch of important reproductive parts? I thought as I shoved my fist into my belly, was there even sperm in me? What did I do in the shower? Why hadn't I checked? What would I do with another woman? To tell someone about my gender just changing was implausible. Nobody would believe me.

"Are you doing okay?" Aurora asked.

I shook my head, no.

"Was it something I said?" I shook my head, no. "Is there something I can do?" I looked at her nervously, finding the words for anything comfortable hadn't found their way to my mouth yet.

She put her hand on mine as she sat next to me. With my thumb, I stroked up and down, once each way. I felt like that was more than I had ever allotted myself to touch a near-stranger, but the selfish act made me feel less sickly.

"We all struggle to not have to struggle," she said to me, eyes sparkling as she smiled patronizingly. I tried to make enough sense of her words to reply, but found myself staying mute. "I know you think everything you touch glitters, and maybe you've been told that in the past, but it simply isn't true. One of these days I think you'll start thinking less of what's going on in the world because of you and start thinking about what's going on inside of you because of the world."

She got up and began preparing mugs and a kettle, leaving the kitchen and dining room momentarily and returning to the table within a minute to show me a locket.

Within it was a picture of a man, with a face much like my own in that it was a man's, but had darker skin and thicker features. He was smiling, had rimmed glasses, and a military-issue hat. I breathed in sharply as I looked to her. She looked away, went to the kitchen, and brought out two mugs of tea. I had become restless while waiting and she noticed my tapping fingers and jittering foot.

She inhaled and spoke quickly. "He wasn't killed in the war," she said. "But he acquired PTSD and took his own life. He was my husband and for a long time I lived in the shadow of fear that I had failed him. Life is terrible to us, even when we give life everything we can."

I gripped her hands with mine and looked at her strong face. Her eyes intermittently sparkled with tears, but her jaw set sternly and she shook her head, smiling bravely.

"We have a long while left to talk," I said.

She brushed her hand across her cheek and said, "The story is a long one."

"Please tell me," I said.

"Well, Ive already given you the short version, but it feels like I'm honoring him to tell all that happened."

She pushed her hand onto the table and began speaking, "Perhaps we all know that we want to be back home, underneath it all. Underneath the layers of loathing and arrogance, we are eager to feel at least some of the comforts we once knew. Perhaps you, sitting silently as the world around you moves, thinking you will find some comfort in traveling, want to believe me, but cannot."

I dipped my head down as I reflected and she spoke on, "Perhaps you went through some traumatic experiences in your home, but I bet you would give up many things in order to go back to your home and correct those wrongs. Truthfully, you want to feel the warm embrace of your parents- because we all have parents, even if we'd like to pretend they ceased existing. Truthfully, you want to be back home. They are more real to us than anything else in this world.

"Pleasures of life are fleeting and restless. They leave quickly. They leave just after you open up a place inside of your heart or brain or wherever you choose to keep them.

"Pain in life seems immovable. Once it has found a place in you- whether you're five, ten, or twenty- it stays, doesn't it? The origin of pain in your life will always be imposing on you. There really is nothing for me to tell you about this. It exists. It is there. It is terrible, but so are we. Humans, awful aren't we?" she shook her head and her ringlets and curls swayed around her shoulders.

"We wage war. War. For a time, ending in 2010, the word 'love' was used more than 'war' in books. They equaled one another for a time until the word 'war' won out against 'love.' We wage war and we have fun doing it. Maybe not as a collective. As a collective, we hate it. But, individuals. Individuals know how to hog-tie a civilian, put their boot on their limp body, and pose for a picture. Fun. The collective gasps when they see this," she shook her head, forgetting her words and simply showing sadness with a furrowed brow and slight frown.

She raised her head and said, "The collective is ashamed that they have ever done something remotely close to this. The individuals in the collective hate that they can remember a time when they held power over someone else. It is a fraction as disturbing as the aforementioned hog-tied, electro-shocked, tortured civilian incident, but they feel guilt for what they've done. The more important the stimulant is, the more neural mechanisms will be activated in order to process the stimuli. The individual will listen to something an individual did and, the more relevant it is to the collective, the more they will relate it back to their own lives. They take fault in that incident. They feel guilty and therefor, strip their own power.

"It would not be so bad if you were just home. It's no doubt that we want to go back to a child-like state. It's no doubt we want to go home, where our self-concept is not in a large part determined by how we identify with our countrymen. If we let the South secede, replaced our congress, then allowed proportional representation with a more parliamentary balance of power of separation, would you feel better about yourself?

"I don't think wishing for the opposite of this one is the way to get what you want," I told her.

"Don't lie, come on. If we had a working government, you would feel better about yourself. You might start to think about having children, or treating the ones around you like they're not entering a false education system, then a market doomed to collapse, inside of a discriminatory system of privilege."

"I don't think I would feel better about myself, though," I protested.

"This is a story, though. It is a story about a soldier. A soldier that wanted to go home without consciously knowing it. I had to explain some of the things that this soldier subconsciously wanted to know would be better. This soldier, Luke Moore, grew up with a mother that remarried several times before staying with a man named Jack that was fat and sold some sort of thing through his small business. Jack had some pairs of plastic glasses with red and blue lenses that I found once. I painted the frames white and wore them once or twice, but like most things that have been stolen, they were immediately tarnished with my initial thievery of them and I hated wearing them. That is the last I'll mention of Jack. Odd man, that one."

She moved her hand around the table and breathed in, "Luke lived with his grandmother, as well, and it was his duty to change her bedpan. I will say no more about the subject, except that Luke only ever mentioned this when he was extremely distraught. His mother was once the second-best boxer in the world. Ask me who the first was," she pushed her face towards mine.

I held up my hands. "I couldn't tell you."

She smiled and said, "Her sister. They were, apparently, quite the team. She, at this stage of her life, looked beaten. In her cheap apartment close to the elementary school he had gone to, working a cheap job, with a cheap husband, and a frustrated son. He worked at a DollarStore when we were teenagers. He got me a job there," she started smiling widely, "And on the first day, I found the hidden place where the opened bags of individually wrapped candy were stored and ate too many to be of any use as a worker. I was too high-energy after that to learn another thing. I never quit and they never fired me, but I had him pick up my only day's check for me.

"Luke was a very frustrated boy. He was becoming a man. A few months after we had become friends, he called me over. I sat on his bed and he described how he had called a girl we both knew. Red haired, beautifully bodied, with a knack for aggression and violence. She had once beaten her fists against me after I had called shotgun and tried to get in the front seat of a friend's car. Crazy woman, and he had asked her to take his virginity and she had."

"He was everything I've said he is and more. He skateboarded, but did not surf. He made everything a joke, but did not tell any actual jokes. He smoked cigarettes, but not weed. He was good friends with the parents of his friends. He was all of these things, and perhaps that is the strangest thing, that he was so much. He wasn't going anywhere and I never questioned it.

"That Luke, he found out how to be a graphic designer, then his red-headed friend taught him how to work computers even more, then she moved on from him and Luke joined up with the army. He grew distant after he signed. Telling friends and family was less fortuitous than he had hoped. They questioned him, told him his decision was ill-conceived. They put him down for such a decision and I couldn't side with either party well enough for his taste. I had always seen myself going into the air-force, but there was a minor medical condition that I had, vaso vagal, that prevented me from undergoing physical stress without the slight probability that I would pass out. Imagine me in an aircraft, adept and skillful, deftly switching the keyboard and then I get pushed by g-force in just the wrong way and I'm nosediving and boom!" she smiled vaguely, not really committing to the emotions behind it.

"Him, I was proud of him for finding a way to become selfless. Not proud enough, I suppose. I may have acted more jealous than I perceived and put him off that way. In any case, he and I grew closer than ever before in the months leading up to his deployment. We were so close, but so far away before he was even gone.

"Basic training was cruel to him. He didn't expect what he was given. Did he push past it or did he succumb? The answer is difficult, but he would not have gotten to Afghanisan if he hadn't pushed past it. He found in himself the critical elements to his success, and held onto them.

"Then he became good. Some visitors to Jerusalem become copiously obsessed with the city and wear a toga, sing hymns, or give sermons. Something like forty people per year come down with this. We're all from that central part of the world, in my belief, and he just fell into a way of doing things, like a visitor to Jerusalem singing hymns, he started doing the things that were expected. Doing them well. Advancing quickly.

"I guess he confused the place he grew up in with the place he was, they weren't completely dissimilar. He cruised the desert as a young professional and servant to the country. He did the awful things that were expected of him and nothing more. He did not put his boot on a twitching, foul-smelling, citizen of the country he was occupying. Like the rest of us, though, he felt like he already had because those that came before him chose to.

"Was it dumb-luck or ultimate destiny that led to what's next? Is it ever either of those two things, or is it something else completely intangible to our brains? Was it his own self-fulfilling prophecy or the way events unfold of their own free-will? He wore lenses that kept everyone at a distance, was it those that kept him from seeing the bomber?"

I gasped and she pushed through words with eyes forced on a place very far away, "They say that in 99% of suicide-bomber cases, the decapitated head of the bomber is intact. It can be found among the rubble and chaos. Something, some trick of physics or some trick of theirs, I do not know what it is, keeps their face and brain and skull completely whole in its gruesome entirety. I want to know what their expressions are. Do you find this face and just know they were contented in that moment of mass killing and destruction? Do they have looks of disgust, at those they are killing or the people they are? I do not know. I have never been in the desert countries between two continents. I don't know.

"He was sent to the army base's hospital within hours, along with several of his platoon. He was there, in a drug and shock induced coma, for a week before being awoken. His mother, of course, knew. Her heart raced between imminent death and a faith in modern science. Would he live or would he die?

"When he woke up, he was back in my San Diego. He was where he had grown up, in the hospital where he had been treated for a sprain. He was where he was not, really. Some people that undergo brain damage like his believe that the hospital they are in is in their home town." She got up, holding onto the back of the chair with a clenched fist before she went to a curio cabinet and pulled from its base an accordion file. Her fingers worked quickly and then she found a piece of paper. She put everything but it away and pushed the form across the table to me and I read it.

TRANSCRIPT OF ARMY DOCTOR'S VILLERY'S
PSYCHIOLOGICAL EVALUATION WITH LUKE
MOORE;

2/14/2022

DR: WHERE ARE YOU, NOW?

TM: THE HOSPITAL.

DR: WHICH CITY ARE WE IN?

TM: SAN DIEGO AND KABUL.

DR: I SEE, AND WHAT STATE?

TM: CALIFORNIA AND AFGHANISTAN.

DR: You are not a soldier in the Afghan war?

TM: No, I am.

DR: And where is that?

TM: Afghanistan, my platoon is stationed in Kabul.

DR: And are you there with them?

TM: Yes.

DR: You are in the army veteran's hospital in Kabul.

TM: Right.

DR: So, California?

TM: I am there.

DR: And the army hospital in Kabul?

TM: I'm there.

DR: Kabul is not part of California.

TM: Yes, it is. We are in San Diego. I am sure it is.

DR: What if we told you that you were in Kabul, in San Diego?

TM: I am.

DR: Doesn't it seem strange that you are in two places, then?

TM: Well, it is strange. Afghanistan is in San Diego. Kabul is part of it.

DR: So you never left San Diego?

TM: No, I did, to go to Afghanistan.

DR: But you said Afghanistan is in San Diego.

TM: I still had to leave it to get there. Kabul and San Diego are two different places.

DR: So, you are telling me you are in both places?

TM: It's something the government did or my wife set it up or something.

DR: So you do not know why you are in two places right now?

TM: No, I don't. Did they tell you, doctor?

DR: They did not because we are not. Take note that the patient exhibits a rare condition associated with damage to the right hemisphere, which he has sustained.

TM: Thank you, doctor. Where did my grandma go?

DR: What do you mean?

TM: This was her room, before I went to war.

DR: Please have him transferred in order to perform CAT-scans and MRI on the patient's right hemisphere and frontal lobe and have copies sent to both of my offices. Thank you, Luke, I look forward to talking to you, again.

TM: Will you get my mom when she comes home?

DR: I'LL TRY.

TM: ARE YOU FROM HERE?

DR: I AM AMERICAN, LIKE YOU.

TM: NO (LAUGHS) SAN DIEGO IS IN
AMERICA.

DR: YOU SAID WE WERE IN AFGHANISTAN.

TM: YES. HEY, ARE YOU SLEEPING IN MY
ROOM? NO WORRIES IF YOU ARE, SINCE I'M
IN MY GRANDMAN'S ROOM.

DR: WE ARE IN AGHANISTAN, NOT YOUR
FAMILY'S HOME.

TM: THIS ROOM, THIS WAS HERS. THIS IS MY
HOMETOWN THAT WE'RE IN. IN AFGHANISTAN.

DR: YOU DO NOT FIND IT UNSETTLING THAT
YOU ARE IN TWO PLACES?

TM: NO, I DO. I FIND IT VERY UNSETTLING.

-END-

I looked at her, deliberately reading her face as
she looked away from the paper, then again at it as
she took it from my hands and stood, to file it away.

"What happened after that?" I asked.

"They kept on like this until they sent him back
home."

"What was that like?"

"It was like trying to pull someone out of a maze.
He was stuck in this labyrinth his mind had made up
that included two different places into one."

I wanted to ask if she had ever found a way, but
my mind halted as I remembered she had said he
had committed suicide.

"Then, eventually," she rubbed her palms together, "I went back home, up here."

"You are a wonderful woman," I said as I looked into her eyes.

"And you are a good man," she said and I looked down ashamedly.

I felt a chill as I said,"I think it's getting late."

"Oh," she said, surprised as she closed the locket and put it in a pocket of her sweater. "In that case, would you like to share my bed with me?"

A blush must have risen to my cheeks as I shook out inappropriate thoughts, "I really couldn't."

She looked at me and pouted her lips, "Why not?"

I tried to truly think of a good reason but couldn't. I had to remind myself that my belief was that sexualization didn't help anybody. I was getting conflicting sensory data, but I had to evaluate that later.

Tomorrow, when I planned on leaving this town, would be a good time to do that. Was there a reason for leaving town, I asked myself, if there was work and friendship here?

I shook my head at Aurora, "I really know it's for the best. I started this whole journey wishing people would stop sexualizing me and I just can't keep up with that cycle."

"Who said anything about sex?" She asked. I wished I could look at her face and judge how she was feeling, but I couldn't keep my head up.

"I guess I did," I said.

"It seems you think a lot of yourself. You'll make an easy target being like that, you know. Everybody knows how to appeal to somebody that likes themselves most of all." She said quickly, glossing over her first statement, "Well I guess that you can take the couch. Blankets are in the trunk next to it," as she padded away and up the stairs.

I sighed as I moved away from the table.

I wanted her, I knew that by my time in the shower, but I had lied and grown indignant. Perhaps I was trying to please her. Perhaps I was finding a roundabout way of pleasing myself. Regardless, I questioned what it says about my inner thoughts if they are not nice enough for other people to know them.

Though I wanted it, I was still averse to the idea. I was not put on this earth to be touched, I was put on this earth to inhale and exhale. That was all there could be to it. Just breathing in and out. As long as I breathed, I had purpose. A hand or groin is not what gave me purpose.

And yet, there I was, creating a place in my thoughts. I was needing to not need it. I was giving it purpose.

"I would call you a cunt," I said to myself, "but you don't have the depth or warmth of one."

I had done something, I realized, to upset myself. Perhaps that is why I was trying to abstain from delving into Aurora.

I heaved my tired body onto the couch.

I had disappointed myself by unwittingly imposing my desires on Aurora, the very thing that upset me. There was a possibility that she did have ulterior motives to get me in her bed. The idea of either one of us urging the other to do something regretful pushed at my conscience. I struggled with the opposing theories until I resolved myself, determining that I was more comfortable sleeping alone.

A moment's thinking told me to join her in bed, but I wondered if that would be an act of pity rather than of mutual desire.

I felt guilty for the pity.

Chapter thirteen

The next morning, Aurora was sweet and kind as she woke up after me and filtered into the room with a smile. She took the mugs we had left on the table to the kitchen and began opening a package of crescent rolls to bake.

"Early riser," she said after saying good morning.

"I was just on a farm and would wake up as the rooster began doing his," I made noisy guttural rooster crows. "I would roll over, put my feet in my shoes, and get to work. So I've been waking up pretty early."

She smiled, "Well that's nice."

I smiled, "It was."

The clock ticked. A bird sang outside. We both smiled.

"I'm going to get my stuff together," I said.

She quickly said, "I'm going to get your laundry out of the dryer." We both parted awkwardly.

In the early morning, I saw White Stripe laying on his side, still asleep. I crept up behind him and did as I had done with a clydesdale years ago, I let my body sink to the ground next to him. I wrapped an arm across his back and around his chest. My face buried into his mane and I let the dirt and dust in his hair enter my nose and instill an old yearning for open trails and long rides.

"Hey boy," I said. His head bobbed up, flickering his eyes to me, then brushed back down to the ground. I rested with him awhile, letting the day begin around us. When he began stirring and moving I patted his chest and got up noisily. He hiked his front hooves out from under him and lifted his torso, head, and neck up first. The rest of his body followed. The blanket Aurora had put on him had slipped off in the nighttime and I pulled a curry comb out of the saddle bag to brush off the dirt and grass from his back and sides. The spiral rubber teeth of the curry comb picked up his old skin and hair, too, resulting in grayish brown clumps that I had to knock off on my boots. I put it away and picked his hooves, shoving dirt and rocks out of the places that should be empty and clear. I tucked the metal pick into my pocket and ran my hands up his legs, feeling two cuts on his legs. I sighed and sprayed water from the hose onto the cuts. I rifled in the saddlebag and found antibiotics to apply externally and wraps to keep the dirt and flies out.

We remained unfazed as an earthquake shook the ground around us and made delicate wooden wind chimes clatter together. He rubbed his head against my shoulder when I stepped back to see how the two leg wraps looked on him.

I placed a hand on his nose, "You're a strong pony." He pushed his head against my hand and I said, "Now let's get out of here." I padded away from him and went up the deck steps. Inside, Aurora handed me my cleaned clothes and I took them outside to my bags.

"I'm going to meet back up with Raluca," I told her as I came back up, "but thank you so much for your hospitality. It meant so much to me when I needed it most."

I looked in her eyes and there was some residual pain there when she said, "Do you value me?"

I shook my hair out in my hand, saying, "I do value you, but," I thought out how to best explain this philosophically, "that is neither true nor false. You are true. That should be and is all that matters."

She cocked her head to the side before smiling and sweeping me in for a hug, whispering, "You're a good man."

I patted her back and sighed, saying, "Thank you, really."

Saddling up White Stripe, I thought about the values I had had instilled in me throughout life. If what I had said was real and values were neither true nor false, then what I had been taught was not really something I needed to hold onto. Values and beliefs were nothing, really, and didn't need to dictate how I felt and behaved.

I led White Stripe out, touching his sides with the backs of my ankles once I had gotten on him, and cantered all the way to the headlands. I staked White Stripe up where he wouldn't destroy the bluffs with his weight and skipped toward the black dot that must have been Raluca.

When I got to him, I said, "I found out your name is Raluca. Mine is Ashna."

"Oh," he said, "odd to have not said such pleasantries before, eh?"

I gave a curt nod and looked towards the bowling ball beach, squinting to see a brighter version today in the light of day. The glowing algae was gone, but the spheres were still in their many rows. I began counting the edges to try to count the total again, but I looked to Raluca, instead. He was smiling and spooling up fishing line when I looked back at him. I squatted next to him, feeling the pervasive wind passing over my shoulders and wrapping around my chest.

He looked up at me and I got the idea we were both waiting for something, "Oh yes," he said as he dug into his pocket and began counting out bills. He handed me four hundred dollar bills.

"Wow," I said softly.

He nodded happily, "It is dangerous work and you did it well."

"You know, I wanted to know what you do with the big pearls. The best ones," I said with an air of question to my tone.

He looked at me with a skeptical eye, "I have already used it."

"No, no. I don't want it," I emphasized the words, "I was just curious."

He looked me up and down and nodded. He rolled up the line from his pole and secured his equipment. He began walking away and I followed.

"Where's your horse?" He asked.

"This way," I said and led him. When we got to White Stripe he raised the stake and glided into the saddle. He patted the small area behind him and I bobbed on my foot before haphazardly jumping up.

"Hiya!" He yelled as he snapped the reins.

I was sent back and had to concentrate hard on not bouncing too high and hurting White Stripe as my butt and tailbone dropped back down. Raluca steered him and his frame blocked my vision from seeing where we went.

He grunted, steering us up a small grassy hill until we were on a plateau and nearly under a brilliant, shining, opalescent gate. He dismounted and I moved up on the saddle. I looked around the long terreplein, which was covered with a thin grass like that found around the flag on a golf course. A slight embankment led up to the flat top on all four sides and the short grass led into tufts of pillow grass and nothing more. The sparse vegetation made the wind race through the area without any hurdles or obstacles and I gripped my clothes around my neck with one hand and steadied White Stripe with the other as he was pushed and pulled by the high velocity winds.

CHAPTER FOURTEEN

He held up a hand, "Stay there," asking me to wait. I looked to the pale, iridescent arch. It was twenty or thirty feet tall, as tall as the depth we had dove last night. Its columns were thick and not engraved or chiseled, but cleanly cut and had perfectly rounded edges.

Raluca approached it, arms outstretched, "This is what became of that itty bitty beauty!" He yelled ecstatically.

A chill ran up the length of my spine and White Stripe pranced in place. I wrapped my fingers around the thin leather of our reins, staring at Raluca. Genuine pride emanated from him, solidifying my intuition that he was being earnest with me.

"In no world could you-" I began, before biting my tongue. He had done something immense. I kicked White Stripe forward and asked, "What is it?"

He shook his outstretched hand, palm towards me, "Don't go under it, don't!"

I caught my breathe, "But why?"

He looked stern as he dropped his hand to touch White Stripe, and I remembered Aurora telling me he was creating gates to heaven. I had told her I didn't believe in heaven. Beliefs could be true or false. My belief could have been wrong. Feelings and values are neither true or false, but beliefs and descriptions could be.

I could have been wrong, I thought as Raluca turned to face the gate. I thought deeply about giving up my beliefs, assumptions, and opinions. They hadn't served me well. I had forced myself out of the real world because of them. I slumped in my seat, shaking my head and frowning.

I had believed I would be imposed on by over-sexualizing men. I had believed it so fully that I was ready to run into the woods and likely die. I had believed it so fully I was afraid to talk to the amazing man that had caught White Stripe. I had let my experience affect my feelings. But those feelings were wrong. Nobody was intending to hurt me. I was hurting myself by being afraid more than they ever could.

"What happens if I go under it?" I asked.

Raluca turned to me, "This is one of the pearly gates, it is," he looked at it and smiled to me, "Heaven."

I looked at him with a smile, "I don't get it, explain."

He shrugged, "There is no explanation. It is not what you would call 'normal.'"

"This world isn't normal," I said.

"Most people think it is," he said.

"I don't want to be here anymore," I said, softening my eyes to look at the smooth, shiny surface of the gate. "I want to try it," I told Raluca.

He looked wide-eyed to me, then the gate, "I do not know how," he said.

"That's okay, I do." I turned at the waist and rifled in my saddlebag, pulling out the rippled bottle I had used to jump through the creek with White Stripe. It felt light in my hands. I opened it and kicked White Stripe forward. He reared, bashing the air with his hooves before springing forward and ripping the earth from under us. He pushed his head and threw his body forward.

I dumped the bottle's liquid fire out in front of us as we passed under the tall gate. It fell from my hand and I watched it drop as a great expanse of nothingness overtook the short grass. It fell to the ground as we fell below ground level. My body felt nothing as our bodies turned down and we fell into the empty space below us. I saw nothing while my eyes took in what felt like lights all around me. I closed my eyes, then opened them, but no new images came to me. I bent at the waist and gripped White Stripes mane as I felt our bodies tumble and turn in the dark. I pressed my torso against his spine, willing my lungs to hold themselves closed as my instincts asked me to scream and shriek. I could feel White Stripe cock his head to look at me, but it flopped to the other side as he turned again in the darkness. I buried my nose in his mane, smelling all of the dirt and fresh scents that were no longer around us. I wished to hit something, anything solid, and to be out of the darkness.

When I did, I had reason to scream. We had hit something, and his body was pressed against my leg. I pushed against the saddle with my hands. I unhooked my top foot from its stirrup and pulled the other free.

"White Stripe, boy?" I hurried around him to hold his head. It was limp and motionless. "What?!" I exclaimed, putting it in my lap. I stroked it from the ear down his cheekbone to the open mouth. It was huge against my small legs. It was huge and so much more important than my tiny body. I inhaled sharply, letting wet tears create rivers down my face and inhaling sharply.

"Whatever you want, you get, but there are always consequences," came a voice.

"No!" I screamed, rocking his head in my hands. "He's still here!"

"Look at me, he's not here."

I didn't look at anybody. I screamed again.

"Would you listen to me?" The voice said.

"No." I stroked his eyelids and tucked my nose into his forelock. I felt a pressure on my forehead and looked up. It was me, the me I had seen in the mirror before White Stripe. "Oh."

"You're something else," she said. "Why would you ever think you could kill him?"

"I'm terrible, I just keep hurting everyone I love."

"Is this what this has been all about?' She asked, seeming very concerned as she put a hand under my chin and began wiping my tears. I looked down at his limp body and she continued, "You keep thinking you're powerful enough to affect every single person on the planet, little thing, but you're the only person that you can change."

"I did change," I laughed through the residual sadness, ebbing it away.

"Yeah you did," she said through the side of her mouth. "Walk with me."

I nodded and looked around as I got up. The sky and ground was all white and only branchy, black trees perforated the perfection. She held my hand and I studied both of them. They were exactly the same size and shape.

"Am I a girl again?" I asked.

"What, not yet a woman?" She asked with a sly smile, "Yes. But this is your heaven."

"So it is real."

"Is it?" She asked, scrunching up her nose, "I wouldn't call it that."

"Oh," I said, confused. "Then-"

"Shhhh," she put a finger to my mouth and said, "you think too much and not very well."

"Oh, well thank you," I put emphasis on my words, "very much. Kind of you to say to yourself."

"You think I'm you?" She asked. She laughed and said, "Have you been paying attention at all? You fell into my domain and I simply took the form most recognizable to you."

I retracted my hand, "Who are you?" I looked at the jawline, shoulders, and eyes that were so familiar, disgusted with them.

"I should leave you in the dark," she said, shimmering into a dark, shadowy version of myself.

I said, "Don't think I don't think. I do, I'm one smart cookie cutter and I could mess you up."

"Could you, now?" She said, a hand raising to her hips, "Slow down, lone wolf. Stop snarling."

I cocked my head, listening. She squinted at me and snapped her fingers. We were sitting in the living room of my parents' home.

"Is this what you're afraid of?" She asked. I saw my mom enter the room, then leave distractedly. I shook my head, "Don't bring her into this."

I heard a cough from the other room and the figure of myself next to me said, "That's how it all starts, isn't it?"

I closed my eyes, "Don't do this, not here."

"How about this?" she said as she snapped her fingers and we were in a lecture hall at my old school. I shook my head again and she snapped. We were standing amid thousands of strangers in a busy square of a big city. I turned my head to the sky, feeling pressed against and scared.

"I don't get it, I really don't," she said. "Nobody's hurt you, so why are you scared?"

I looked at her, "What if they do?"

"They don't. Who has the power to hurt, wolf?"

"I do," I told her.

"Who?" she yelled.

"Me, it's me!" I yelled back, "I'm the wolf! I'm the one messing people up. I'm the one imposing on them! I'm the one with bad values! I'm the problem, not them!"

"Why is your family an exception?" She asked.

"They will always be proud and happy," I said.

"Why are your teachers an exception?" She asked.

I gasped and shrugged, "They're paid to be proud and happy."

She jutted her chin -my chin- and asked, "Who are you?"

"A wolf."

She asked, "A lone wolf?"

"Hopefully," I said.

She glided around me and asked, "Why?"

I shrugged, "So I don't hurt anyone else."

She touched my face, moving hair away from my eyes, "Not quite."

I couldn't think.

"Think," she said.

I couldn't talk.

"Tell me," she said.

I couldn't breathe.

"Don't die on me," she said. I clutched my stomach, doubling over and finding myself against the white ground, spitting up blood. It came out of me fast and my eyes lingered on it.

I looked away from it, only to see my father's bent head. His straight black hairs were marred and glistening with oils and from just under them, I could make out the bands of fatigue sprouting from under his eyes. I reached out to hold his hand and he looked up at me, brown eyes sparkling as he forced a smile. He was ready to cry, as was I. He opened his mouth and I knew what he was going to say as I looked at the body we were both bent over. She had just been coughing. There was blood on her white bed sheets.

He had told me she would be all right.

I was gone from them, though. I was gone from my brothers, both curled in a love seat in the corner of the hospital room. I was gone from my father, working hard to push us away from the past. I was not gone from my mother, though, because she had left before I had the chance to do so, first.

"Why?" The figure asked, circling around me on the white floor. She was momentarily blocking my vision of the scattered black branches and trees, and, of course, the limp, inert body of my horse.

I spat, "Why what?"

"Why are you alone?"

I said, "I don't want it, okay?"

She said, "Oh yes you do. People want you, that's a problem for you. So why are you still alone?"

"Because I have sharp teeth, I don't know."

I could feel her breathing in my ear, "You're no better off than you were before you were a man."

I trembled, "No, that's not-"

She cut me off, "Yes."

"No, that's not true."

"The point of having beliefs is to find truths," she said, "and you're just as ignorant to the truths as ever. So why do you believe that you're all the wiser?"

I struggled to grip what I had once known, letting words stumble out of my mouth, "No belief is knowledge."

"Because knowledge is 100% certain, I know. I didn't ask you what you know. I want to hear what you believe is true, because that is where this fallacy started."

Overwhelmed by my grief for White Stripe and my mother, I spat at her form.

"Who do you think you are?" She asked, "Do you think you're good enough? For this? For all of this?" She spread her arms around her. She sounded like someone I had known.

The hostility I was faced with inside me burned until I screamed, then calmed me.

"This isn't heaven!" I yelled before I had to double over again, blood smattering the white ground around me. In my disorientation I thought to keep the blood from touching White Stripe's large, brown body. "This isn't heaven," I said again as I wiped the blood from my mouth.

She quickly approached me, "You're right, you're not good enough to go there."

She sounded like someone from my childhood, but the idea that I recognized her voice slipped from my mind's grasp. As I searched my mind for who it was, I forgot altogether that it could have been anybody.

"Get away from me." I spat blood at her as I spoke.

"You are in my castle," she said to my face, "treat it as such. Do you get it, that you can't get to the perfect world? That there is no perfect world and that wishing for the opposite of the one you're in won't work?"

"There has to be some way-" I started to say but she turned her back on me, laughing.

"No, trust you me, there is not."

"Well, then why be in this world?"

"You mean your world. What did it ever do to you?"

"What it does to billions of girls and women everywhere, and boys and men. There are these systems that oppress."

"You want to talk about systems?" she asked, cocking her head as she looked at me again, "You want to talk about good and bad? Right and wrong? You want to talk about rabble-rousing rhetoric, barriers, suppression, hate and terror in your little world? You think humans fighting other humans is really the worst thing out there? Don't you?"

"It's not the absolute worst, but-" she held up a hand and I stopped talking.

"You know what you humans get?"

I shook my head, "No."

"Aw, come on. Don't be scared," she didn't make any pretense to act kindly or change her body language. "It's no fun for me if you're too afraid to speak."

I offered, "We get thought."

"Aha! And what is thought?"

I bit my bottom lip.

"It is pattern detection. Now, extend that to your own life. What is the pattern there?"

I thought of my mother being gone when I was young and my father working hard, gone in his own way. I thought of then women, men, and friends that had come and gone in my life. Bitterly, I said, "Loneliness."

"That's why we're good for each other," she said, pointing a finger in the air.

The anger in me growled, and I lunged at her, but she side-stepped me with words streaming from her mouth, "There is no good or bad way of looking at the world, so I won't fault you for hating it, but-" I shot my body at her again, trying to make her at least vanish for a moment. I wanted a second away from her. Seamlessly, she spoke, "-the cost of rationality is that thinking takes time. I'll give you some time, to be fair to you, you little thing."

I inhaled and she laughed, slowly dissipating into the white background. I looked around, desperately alone.

CHAPTER FIFTEEN

"Ayo!" came the diminutive man's voice. My face felt like a burning book had slapped it as his hand met my cheeks. "Wake," another slap, "up!"

"All right, all right!" I said, rising.

"Not of this world, eh?"

I shook my head, "Where is he?" I asked.

Raluca shrugged, "No idea."

"You can't be serious."

"He's not here."

I looked around the terreplein. The grass swayed methodically in the wind, but White Stripe's body was nowhere.

My face felt itself contort, and Raluca threw himself around me as my shoulders bobbed forward and sharp, wheezing sobs left my chest.

"No!" I screamed, but the wind seemed to take my words away from me too quickly. I was on the ground, pounding the earth, screaming, "This couldn't have happened! He's not gone, he's there, he's under us!" I saw Raluca moving about me, showing concern in small hand gestures and sounds like doves cooing. My teeth felt like they would be thrown from my body as I screamed and tears rolled down my cheeks, "I said, no!"

"Nothing changes, now. The change is done. Come back with me, you need to rest." My head shook and my body trembled, but he guided me by the elbow and hand. After a mile's walk, I was reduced to quietly whimpering as we returned to the northwestern cove. As we approached the town, he surveyed me and smeared a thumb across the bottom of my eyes and smiled into my eyes.

"Let me ask you," he said, "are you still here, alive, on this planet?" I shrugged my shoulder and twisted my head to look away from him. "Yes!" he exclaimed, "You are very much alive," he poked me sharply as he spoke, making me recoil and hold my elbow with one hand. He led me towards Aurora's house. He knocked fast and lightly, standing rigidly at the door. I could feel his unease radiate from him in the moment of silence before we heard feet hitting the floor on the other side of the door. When he heard her approaching the door, he looked at me jovially. Something in his happy smile made my jaw jut outwards and tears spring to my eyes.

Aurora's eyes sparkled as she opened the door, "Hello, oh-" her voice tapered drastically as she saw me and as her body moved forward to hold me, mine collapsed in her arms. I felt the soft, dry skin of one of her breasts and, after just a moment of my face being pressed against it, felt it become moist and sticky with my tears.

"Oh, my," I heard her say as they both took me inside, "What could have-"

"No," came Raluca's stern voice.

Around me, a blanket fortress was erected.

I ruin everything, I thought.

"Lift up," Aurora said. I lifted my neck and she placed a pillow under my head. "Another," she said and I did the same and she did the same and I rolled onto my side. Something in my pants hurt as I laid on it and my hand pushed into my jeans to get it. In my hand was the doll, with its red corduroy shirt and blue pants that I had found. His little face smiled up at me and my mouth opened to breathe. A small sob shook me, for I noticed the way his happy face was so dissimilar from mine.

"Oh, you poor thing," she said, and I pushed the doll and my hands down, gripping the place in between my thighs and the soft clothe of the doll.

Nothing was impervious to my stain, I said to myself.

I stayed like that, rocking in a fetal position until the light had faded and I knew that it was night. I turned over, staring at her house's ceiling, trying to discern pattern from isolated randomness. Her corgi came up and licked my face and I didn't move at first. It wiped my nose with its tongue and rubbed its own nose against my ear. It was such a cold shock, but I remained still. Aurora approached me and rubbed my hair with her hand, bringing my head to her chest and lulling me to sleep.

CHAPTER SIXTEEN

The sun moved slowly over my face and my sleep chose to ignore its presence on my skin. In dreams I was mildly aware that I was avoiding something, but I conceded that I simply didn't want to wake. So often, I had chosen to sleep in. So often, and with a father that routinely took long shifts and wasn't there in the mornings to wake me, I would sleep until the last possible moment.

Rolling out of bed, I would slip on shoes and grab my backpack. Maybe that's why I was such a good student, I thought. I didn't put in any work in the mornings to look good, like the other girls. Without anything like good looks to fall back on in school, I had chosen to excel in my studies, instead. Maybe, I thought, it was a good thing that I didn't have any parents pressing me to get up.

I smiled as I thought this, the faux-happiness waking me. I stretched my arms out, disheveling the pillows and blankets that had been built up around me.

I ran to the backyard and, gripping the wood of the porch, breathed in softly. The smell of horse poop was a comfort. I looked around to a mirror that stood on the porch, cocking my head to the side as I saw the woman's face and body I had once been used to.

"Back to normal," I said and I breathed in heavily, looking at the parts of the grass where hooves had pushed into it, creating indentations. I leaned on the banister heavily, letting my head fall into my elbow.

"I heard you get up," Aurora said from behind me. I lifted my head. "Thought you might want this." She handed me a warm cup and I touched it to my mouth.

I gulped and said, "Thank you, for everything."

"It isn't a problem," she said, turning to look at me. I studied her eyes, seeing storms breaking out of the webs of her irises. I could tell there were tears forming there, hindered by her control, and I wondered if they were there for me or for her own pain.

"I think I'm going to go back today," I told her, "and try to save him."

"Do you really think that's a good idea?" she asked.

"Of course, I have to try. I bet he's there. I should have waited." She placed a hand on mine with a sigh and I exhaled, too, looking off at the layers of clouds in the green sky. "I could try."

"You could," she said measuredly.

I nodded and she watched the white foreground of clouds move both towards us and away, at the same time. The clouds' tumult echoed my own and I let the wind push and sway me as it did to them. I felt Aurora's arm around my back and her hand slipped over my arm. I leaned into her and she set down her coffee to hold me closer. I pressed myself in to smell her chest, a sweet and nostalgic smell I had only smelled in passing. I pushed my nose into it further. Her hand held the back of my hair, almost pushing my face into her.

I breathed in, deeply, trying to fill my lungs with her, but my breathe faltered and spun out of me quickly. Wild elation pulled at my body as it moved into her.

"Oh?" she said as she heard my breath falter and I felt her hand trail down from my head, along my spine, until it rested on the small of my back. Her other hand held the back of my neck as my head cocked to the side. Our mouths met and I tried lapping her up with my tongue, taking from her mouth the tastes of her cheeks and tongue.

She laced her fingers into my hair and stroked it down, giving me shivers down the spine with her affection. My hips pushed into her, feeling the cushion of her body as mine warmed on it. I felt like we were alone, in a movie theatre, watching ourselves projected in front of us.

"Did you want that to happen to begin with?" I asked her.

She paused in her finger-combing to answer and I deeply regretted causing her to stop, "I did, but you didn't seem interested."

"Well, I didn't want to take advantage of you," I explained. I looked up at her, trying to grasp and attach myself to the scene we were in together. I felt awkwardly detached from the experience.

"Now why would you think that?"

"I want to treat you like a person, not the sum of your experiences. But, as a man, it seemed like a very easy thing to do with you."

She betrayed no offense in her face, but spoke cuttingly, "So women that are easy are a thing to you?"

"No, no. I can't believe I said it like that. You're right, you know you're right and I wish I was right, too. For your sake."

"Your apology is enough, and I even think I know where you're coming from. Being a widow has never been easy, but it is especially hard when people treat me warily, like I'm a broken object that could get hurt easily."

"Well, what if they're just reflecting onto you how they really feel?" I said, thinking I may have done that.

She sighed, looking at me.

I said, "I'm still so naive, even after everything I've been though."

"What have you really been through?"

I was already thinking of a story and told her that instead, "A story from Greek myth about a guy turned into woman, Tiresias, I think, was asked by a pair of Gods which orgasm was better. When he answered that the woman's was, he was blinded by the Goddess and spent the rest of his days a blind prophet." Aurora nodded and the words fell from my lips into her lap, "Even after knowing both genders, I am still naive, just like Tiresias!"

Aurora asked me, "When did you start believing the lies you told yourself?"

"I actively taught myself not to trust others. I made it my goal, as a kid and adult, I guess."

"Well, how have they shaped your experience?"

I laughed and sighed instantaneously, "The things I want haven't been clearer because of them."

"Maybe it's the things you don't want to see that are enhanced?"

I laughed, "That would mean I should just not want anything."

She looked at me, her idea contained concisely in her eyes as she did, "Maybe that's a good idea."

"I've been doing so much to find-" I stopped short.

"Find what?"

"My happiness, I guess."

"And you did that alone?"

I nodded, "I need to do it alone."

"Without thinking anybody was supposed to help you," she said, "while thinking only about your own happiness. Ashna, that's just not how it works. It's a dual effort. You can run around the entire world looking for a big ball of happiness with your name on it, but the more people you ask for help finding it the more likely someone will bring it to you."

I looked at her, grabbing her hand from my head as I did and kissing it, "I'm happy to have you here, searching with me."

She looked at me carefully, "What do you think of the way society will look at you now?"

"I think that society only had faith in itself, not as an individual, which it has faith in as contributor to be a mirror for them. That's it. Nobody really actually had faith in me unless I was showing them," I was at a loss for words and said, "what they wanted to see."

"That's an extremely pessimistic view of other people."

"Well maybe it's time the general mindset was replaced with some pessimism."

Aurora sighed into her arm and adjusted herself to be closer to me, "You'll hurt yourself thinking like that. In twenty years, you're going to be really tired thinking like this. You might even have done a number of drugs in order to not think like this."

"No," I shook my head, "never."

I looked up to see she had a look of skepticism. "Why is it you think that you're better than the rest of the world? Nobody asked you to get on that high horse." I looked at her, shocked, "I'm so sorry, I am," she said. "Now that you're up on it I don't want to see you get knocked off of it, that's what I meant, but I shouldn't have said that."

"I'm so unhappy," I said.

"Besides your horse, why are you unhappy?" she asked, eyes adjusting to look at different parts of my face.

There was nothing more than, "Because I am unhappy."

"What is it like?" she whispered.

"Like I'm drowning inside my own mind."

"Well, what's your mind's oxygen?"

"It's the same as everyone's: happiness."

She sighed heavily and looked at me for a long time while brushing my hair with her fingers. She finally said, "You can be broken up and hurt all over and you can become better from that," she said.

"I don't know if I can fix this broken mess," I said.

She asked, "Do you want to accept help from someone else?

"You don't want to fix me. Nobody wants to fix other people."

"Sure they do. I do. That's what I'm trying to tell you."

I sighed into her hair, "When you're trying to mend something that's been smashed, the cracked pieces could wound you."

"If that were true, I wouldn't be here," she said.

CHAPTER SEVENTEEN

I was at the bottom of a river, looking up at the brilliant churning and moving of it. I had tied a rope to rocks and held onto them, breathing in the perfluocarbon water second-naturedly. The water swept past me, turning my hair so that it sometimes swept across my face and I could not see the top of the stream. I remembered when White Stripe and I had jumped into the water at the end of the pier and fallen in so that we were walking on it. It all seemed so distant, now.

Bubbles of air escaped from inside my ears and floated upwards before dissipating into the perfluocarbon surrounding me. I watched them until they were gone.

I blinked, slowly feeling detached from even my own body. My eyes seemed to be watching me from above, seeing my body sway and swing with the river water's gentle movement as I held onto the tethered rock, like a child with a balloon.

For months, I had searched. For months, the incessant need to find White Stripe had torn at me. I had gone back to the arches, gone back to the farm, gone back to the park, and gone back to Robert. I had tearfully told him all that I could and he had looked to Aurora, standing near me with a bent head as she perhaps fully understood how confused I had been. Robert and his wife had talked to Aurora as I sat in her car, hands under my face as I cried into them. I was guilty of my recklessness. Aurora had told me little of their discussion, just that he was concerned for me, as was she.

I had her drive by the Lavocaine farm, but the only thing in the paddock he had used were weeds. I had gone back to the park and worried Iliza so much, she pressured Aurora into letting her come to the house. She stayed for dinner twice, sometimes three times, a week. Raluca had me working, diving, often and the tremendous pain of pulling and pushing my body against the cold ocean was the only reprieve to my search. I could not think of anything but the pain of the restless water against me. I could not search for anything else as I searched out oysters. It unfettered me and, though the joys of liberation inhibited me from being cognizantly aware, I was emancipated from the pain of loss when I was in the water.

He pulled me up one night and patted the sharp black rock he was perched on before saying, "I would say it is nice living in a house that has been completely taken hostage by plants, but it was a bit strangling." My ears pricked, listening over the orotund bellows from the gaping mouths of waves perching and crashing below us.

"The house I lived in had grapevines pulling at the windows and falling down the outer walls. Ferns abounded in the corners and on the patio. Dozens of planters littered every room. Not because of that, but just because, there was always good reason to get out of the same old rooms. You would go from one room to the next, going about your business, but eventually you would find yourself feeling the need to get out, breathe new air, which is silly, of course."

He shook his head at the ocean's sparkling face as it swelled and receded, then said, "When I walked between rooms, I dreaded being in the hallways, where people would ask me what I was up to and chase me around. I just wanted to be in one room, then the next.

"It was hard, but yes, that is where I grew up. So when I went into my magical world, going out one door led into another room or building. There was no walking to and fro."

I drew in a breath, having not anticipated a story I could relate to so well. I stood to squat and rubbed on my thighs. He rarely spoke so long and I wanted to encourage the rest of his story to continue, "No going to the market, just being in your room, then being at the market?"

He nodded his head and said, "After you step through your house's ingress, you're out an egress. Very alarming to do that, like living in a dream. The plants were doing all sorts of things, too, because of what people would say."

"I noticed that, too."

He looked at me oddly, "Oh?"

"What sort of things?"

"People had said the plants were choking them before the magic happened, and that they did. Very scary. People had said they would develop minds of their own, which they did, but never talked. Other things, too, minor things that worried and scared me, at first. I learned, though. I didn't change, not the way you did. You are not the person you were a few months ago. Not the same," he paused, "skin."

"No," I said, no emotion left to feel about it.

"After your horse," he said, then stopped short of words.

"My world was so different," he said, "and I still haven't gone back to every little thing being different or the same, but I have found out that family is here, my friends are here. So, I am here."

"That's really important to hear right now," I had said, thanking him. "I never really understood that to face the world, with all of its," my throat caught on what I was going to say, "eccentricities? Hinderances? I don't know what I would call them, but it's much easier to face them with friends."

He nodded, "Very important."

I spent every hour of my time trying to find White Stripe, though. That was the one question Raluca couldn't answer.

I had spent all of my time drawing nearer and nearer to insanity. I had needed him.

As I pulled myself down, fingers wrapping around the waterlogged rope, I realized I did not. Although I was dating Aurora, I didn't need her. I didn't need my old girlfriends or boyfriends, nor did I need Iliza, nor my work, nor did I need White Stripe.

I sighed, the exhalation causing a plume of water to push away from me and rise with the water. The need to find him was gone, as was the need to do anything else.

I untied the rope and pushed against the rocks at the bottom of the river, the chinking sound of their movement coming to my ears as I did. I breathed in again, one last time underwater, before surfacing. I held my breathe until I had swum to shore and bent over, coughing up water and putting my finger to the dangling bag at the back of my throat to vomit it out expertly. As I did so, in a fleeting instant, I got the idea that I had made this world up, as I had wished to change the world into one of opposites with Robert, that had happened through faulty analogies and ad hominem- or damning the source. I had felt so imposed on, that I thought I couldn't let them have an affect on me, but they truly had. I could have made up the entire series of events on a milieu across the West.

I held myself by pushing my palms against my knees and dangled, looking between the back of my legs at the water. Its movement across the rocks and branches of the riverbed created interruptions in its mirroring of the trees and branches above it. I breathed in air and put on my clothes and shoes.

The river meandered through the forest and I followed it, my boots finding the path before my eyes did. I heard the forest around me. Leaves shifted against one another like paper chimes. Boughs and tree limbs creaked like old houses. Birds and small mammals called out to another, usually songs and sounds of warning that I was there. My hands slapped my thighs as I walked and I listened to the rhythm, looking down, trusting my body and the path.

When I did look up, I was startled. I saw a cloaked, hooded figure walking along the opposing bank. I followed the river, watching them always. I was perturbed by them but intrigued beyond measure. I could not take my eyes away and stopped walking completely when they pushed their cloaked, dark feet into the water. The figure stepped in, walking slowly and steadily. The river had pooled here and the qualities of a mirror that the river possessed where made to ripple as it reflected the green branches and trees above it.

I turned into the river, then jumped in, arms pumping the water beneath me. Only then did I think about the opposites of the world. They all seemed to relate. I swam towards the figure as they stood chest-deep in the water. All of the things that had happened in the world of opposites had been said to me before I had met Robert. I slowed, as to not splash the hooded figure as I approached. All of those things that had confused me in this world were specific to me. I stood in the water across from the figure and lifted my hands to the hood. They did not reflect on the world at large, but just on my perception of it. Lifting the hood, I saw the man that I had changed into was standing across from me, looking into my eyes. The world of opposites was not that at all, but a figment of my perception.

The man smiled, nodding his head towards the bank. I heard the sound of hooves, but I did not look away from him. I bowed my head and jumped towards him, hugging him. I turned away and made an effort to jump through the water towards the bank. I laid on my belly and swam, then pushed the ground and ran towards him. He bowed his head, and I rubbed his forelock, weaving my fingers into his long hair and running them downwards, until they pushed against his bridle.

I had imposed. I had, along with everyone else. Like children testing the boundaries, we had pushed the boundaries of people's comforts and seen what we do and don't like to do. How we could all get our way in life without hurting one another while doing it. If Hume taught us rationality is finding the most effective means to an end, and our rational obligations are not absolute, then how long can you carry them out to that end until you begin wondering if they should be changed? I had been so scared to live before, I had been afraid of getting results in order to make observations. Even Bayo, the grimy Lavocaine grower knew that. Even Nycho with his gun and hurt girlfriend knew. Aurora certainly did. I wasn't myself for them; I was guarded and reserved. My true self was saved for talks with White Stripe.

I patted him, unlatching the bridle around his face, then swept it off and hooked it above a broken branch. I went to his girth and unlatched it, then let the saddle and bags fall next to us. He pranced about, lifting his legs high and moving away from me, then forward. I giggled and he snorted, shaking his head and finally becoming still.

I had spent so much energy being alone or riding him that I hadn't let myself be helped by those around me, nor help them. I watched him, but did not move to touch him, again. Instead, I went to the saddlebag and opened it, taking out the gun I had taken from the man I had sent to the farm.

I walked towards the river with it, looking back at White Stripe as he stamped his hoof, watching the water I was going into before I walked in. I took from my pocket the rope and dove under, breathing in the water as I did and choking on it before breathing it in again and being able to take in lungfulls of it. Turning, I saw the watery river, a landscape I knew well, as a completely different place, one where I could live. I kicked to the bottom of the pool and tied the rope around my wrist, then a rock. I looked up at the brilliant, churning movement of the water above me.

I held the gun in front of me, deep green in the short distance to my face, cocking it back. I noticed how the river's water blanched as it receded away from me and towards the bright sun, it's spindly spark was a hint, a suggestion of warmth from up there as I squeezed the trigger. The light glimmered in the distance, fading as it approached me. I saw a burst of liquid flame had shot from the cylinder as its burning gold appearance in the pale indigo waters streaked from the piston's impetus.

The combustion's path that I had seen tearing, recklessly spiraling from it, engulfed the water around me, then dissipated and became transient, fading. Then, fire, caused by the water, tore from the perfluocarbon river any oxygen. I dropped the gun in the rocks at my feet, its descent slowed by the roiling water.

The oxygenated water in my lungs was ripped out of them. I tried taking in lungfuls but it choked me. The sensation was odd and new, wistfully evocative of the life I had once had. Not being able to breathe in the river was nostalgic, like I was back home. The current pushed down, its warm water gently caressing me away from the de-oxygenated and hot water. I began choking up the water and brought my hands behind me, then forward, pushing towards the surface. I pushed against the current and upwards. Though I was perturbed by the sensation, I lived on.

www.ingramcontent.com/pod-product-compliance
Lightning Source LLC
Chambersburg PA
CBHW020235130626
46549CB00005B/1907